good deed rain

Books by Allen Frost

Ohio Trio
Bowl of Water
Another Life
Home Recordings
The Mermaid Translation
The Selected Correspondence of Kenneth Patchen
The Wonderful Stupid Man
Saint Lemonade
Playground
Roosevelt
5 Novels
The Sylvan Moore Show
Town in a Cloud
A Flutter of Birds Passing Through Heaven:
    A Tribute to Robert Sund
At the Edge of America
Lake Erie Submarine
The Book of Ticks
I Can Only Imagine
The Orphanage of Abandoned Teenagers
Different Planet
Go with the Flow: A Tribute to Clyde Sanborn
Homeless Sutra
The Lake Walker
A Hundred Dreams Ago
Almost Animals
The Robotic Age
Kennedy
Fable
Elbows & Knees: Essays & Plays
The Last Paper Stars
Walt Amherst is Awake
When You Smile You Let in Light
Pinocchio in America

Pinocchio in America

Pinocchio in America © 2019
Allen Frost, Good Deed Rain
Bellingham, Washington
ISBN 978-1-64516-987-1

Writing: Allen Frost
Cover Photos: Allen Frost
Cover Production: Jen Armitage
Apple: TFK!
Bird Taxi Illustration: Allen Frost

Quotes from:

Hayden Carruth from *Tell Me Again How the White Heron Rises Across the Nacreous River at Twilight Toward the Distant Islands,* New Directions, NY, 1989

Pinocchio in America, by Angelo Petri, Doubleday, Doran & Company, Inc. Garden City, New York 1928

My Air Armada, by Air Marshal Italo Balbo, Hurst & Blackett, Ltd. London, May 1934

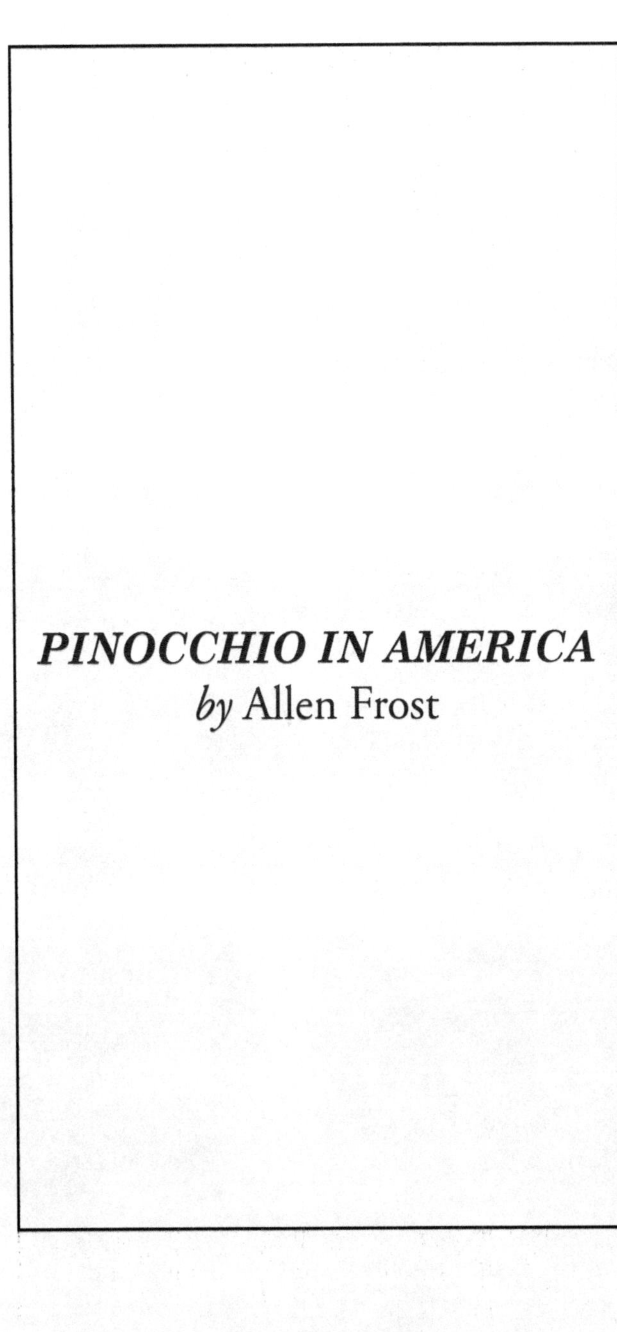

PINOCCHIO IN AMERICA
by Allen Frost

Your minds are the minds of men who feel and imagine without time

—Hayden Carruth

INTRODUCING PINOCCHIO IN AMERICA

This all began with a trip to a local town north of Bellingham. Lynden is the perfect place for Pinocchio to reappear. Windmills, ice cream and elm trees, Norman Rockwell on the corner with his easel; they used to have speakers on the lampposts that would play music above the sidewalk. Front Street, with its bookstores, antique shops, shoe repair and bakeries, but I like the alleys. That's where I found that little house where our hero lives. The cover photos are also from that alley. It's the sort of place where time stands still.

First mention of this book began May 18, 2015 with the words: "Pinocchio's Car Lot" and more ideas continued in my blue notebook through the summer. Then once the novel began, it motored away from these little notes. If I didn't recapture these now, cup them quick in my hands, and pour them into these pages, they would have flown back to wherever they came from. This book was completed almost exactly one year after it started, on May 19, 2016.

All my writing begins in notebooks. I like those little 3"x5" ones you can get in any good store. A lot of the time, before I plunge into a novel, it's the little ideas that form the big picture, or at least take me there. *Pinocchio in America* was no different.

Oftentimes many of these ideas never make it into the final book, but it's interesting to go back to that original notebook and see where Pinocchio could have branched off on other adventures, alternate storylines in a parallel world. They are almost like journal entries, written early in the morning or scribbled quickly at work. They begin September 14, 2015:

Lynden Milan can only speak in the past tense. He stopped by the alley today to turn off the waterline for winter.

Sometimes there are things in the clay—debris, Pinocchio.

An old movie theater can be entered by alley. The street entrance is bricked over. I go in there, run the projector, find a seat and watch movies.

Finds Pinocchio and sets him on a shelf. He doesn't come to life right away.

I can't believe they used to build things this way. What are we doing making things from clay?
—9/16/15

Finds a crystal ball but when he touches it (he can see a vision in it) it pops like a bubble.

A radio station. My pirate radio. An old antenna perched on a roof. There were shelves of records, boxes on the floor. I can play whatever I like. I haven't heard from anyone in town, I don't know if they're listening. Who even listens to the radio anymore? Maybe it's just for me, though I like to think there's someone out there, tuned in. Candles and record players.

I might be the only one to spend time in the alley. Sometimes a Wheel will wander through, but like a big moth trying to avoid entrapment in a web, they will hurry out the next side street they find. I guess it takes a certain person to find beauty here.

I thought about tying the fire escapes overhead to make bridges that would reach over the alley. Wouldn't that be great! Anyway, I don't know how I could do it. Not without cranes and wires and a circus crew. I guess I'm happy just picturing it in my mind. Sometimes I think there's another reality where those things are true. I think them up here and they materialize over there.

—9/16/15, job

An escaped waxwork from the museum: "I was a minor figure in the theater where Abe Lincoln was shot. I was reaching from the curtain, trying to stop it from happening."

—9/17/15, job

KIMONO & SONS

Daniel Fellows, the millionaire who is buying up the town to preserve his childhood.
"Those are the most honest, beautiful days of my life."

"I don't know if this is the answer to a prayer." Watching the old town reappear as it was, as Mr. Fellows restores it.
—9/20/15

I've always been attracted to the past. That's why I live in an alley.

Hears something on the radio, late at night sound drifting across America. No way of knowing where it's coming from…another pirate radio station blowing along out there.
—9/21/15, 6:31 AM

There used to be a milkman who would wander down here, clinking bottles. He knew everywhere in town, everything had a story. When he died, he left the map behind.
—9/24/15, 6:55 AM

There is a diner inhabited by ghosts. I sat down with them, in their midst, and I was served too, a delicious oatmeal with fruit and a thick mug of coffee. At first I thought they were ghosts, old men having breakfast served by an old waitress, but then I realized they were real as me.
—9/24/15, job 11:25

The rocking chair on
top of the fir tree 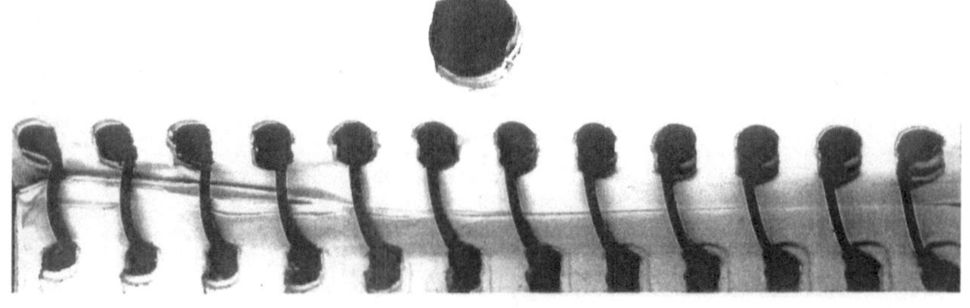

9/25/15   7:08 AM

It wasn't long
after the 20th century
but enough time had passed
to make it seem
like another world
            [way of life]

                    9/28/15

Over on the other side, the stores aren't the same.
What is an old bookstore on my alley side, is a vita-
min supplement store on Front Street.
—10/2/15, 6:18 AM

I can't explain the transformation. Do I need to?
Tic Toc has a light bulb for an eye. He gets bulbs at the
dollar store: "They don't last long, but they're cheap."
—10/2/15, job

orange spark of life in it.
—10/3/15

Tic Toc talking to him and his arm falls off.

He bragged about being state of the art, but I recognized some of his parts as 20th Century. I've seen him
on a tea kettle and his control panel is from a General
Electric range stove.
—10/9/15

a square of silk

Aren't they like whales, these tall fir trees catching the
first white light of day on their skin, standing together
silently?
—10/11/15

Frank Sinatra torch song records: *In the Wee Small Hours, Only the Lonely, Where are You?, No One Cares*

Echo Avenue: footsteps and keys dropped, any words the sounds repeat
>   —10/13/15

AT THE END: I was done with adventures, getting in the flying rowboat

"I don't know how to meet people. I don't know how that aligns itself to happen. Anyway, I wouldn't know what to say if I did."
"Aw, what's that matter with you? It's easy!" Pinocchio snapped his wooden fingers.
>   —10/19/15

Finds a string of twine (it changes color and fiber as he follows it) turns into a cedar cord as he follows it into the woods where there are totem poles. It turns into computer cord as it leads into the city.
>   —10/19/15, 6:30 AM

They go to 1950s style Drive-In, park outside. A young girl comes up to the window. She looked like she was 12. "What would you like to order?" Then she quickly added, "My friends dared me to say that!" He saw the group of teenagers laughing inside at their table.
"I want your mother's phone number!" Pinocchio answered.

—10/20/15

Driving in the countryside, they see a sign for whale watching. There's no ocean for miles, trees, farms, mountains. "Well, I think there's a lake near here"
"That can't be big enough for a whale!"
"That's why we have to go find out."
They pay for tickets and pass the gate, go deep into the woods. They park and follow a trail. They see water. Beside a pond, there's a plywood whale. It says SUCKER on it.

—11/1/15

The air jellies gathered around the caravan and bobbed
around glowing red and blue colors.
                    —11/5/15, from dream

Sign: *You Must Be This Tall To Ride*
"Excuse me, son. You'll have to leave."
                    —11/7/15

Two shady looking characters
approached us, "You need a ticket?"

He catches the Invisible Man in the alley, standing
close to the heating vent. He never would have known
he was there if he wasn't smoking a cigarette.
                    —11/14/15

Old Woman Who Lives in a Shoe: "Sorry I don't have
any food to give you. My kids ate it all."
They visit her later in book. Pinocchio: "Yeah, well I
don't need to eat."
                    —11/15/15

Pinocchio: "You'd rather be in this ghostworld?" Pinocchio gets him to move out of old alley. He moves to apartment in city. Little blank plastic room.
                    —12/4/15, job

This portion of the story had to be recreated using Super-8 film. I have no recollection. I can only watch myself like someone in a dream, or a movie star.
                    —12/8/15

We take Sylvan Moore's car from the lot for a joyride and I let Pinocchio take the wheel. He hits a dog. The owner watched it happen from his porch and calls to us, "It's okay. He's fine. This happens all the time." The dog appears on the porch and watches from the doorway. "Okay," we say and drive away.
                    —12/12/15

In the early morning, a bat flew overhead like some badly hinged toy. It made for a dark barn covered in blackberries.
                    —12/16/15, 8:45 AM cold

The gypsies came to their town, set up a circus and sold them a piano right out of the back of a truck. They made bonfires on the beach when the sun went down and the moon came up and in the starlight they left.

—12/16/15

What happened to Tic Toc's robot Pinocchio? He finds it in the attic behind boxes and cobwebs. He uses it to track down Pinocchio.

—12/20/15

I wanted that talking cricket to show up.

—12/21/15

They walked along the railroad tracks.
"Why don't you walk on the ties?"
"I like these rocks."
Beside the tracks were volcanic-looking stones, brown or black, and pitted like chunks of the moon.
Along the bay, way beyond the posted KEEP OUT signs, the clear lapping water, islands, out to Poe's Point, past the NO TRESPASSING sign.

Pinocchio leads him up onto the roof of [The Leopold] The Cleopatra building. "They used to dock zeppelins here." They climb past the DANGER sign.

Things are going fast now.

Lets Pinocchio drive. "How about I drive with my eyes closed?"

They use a car to go to the author's house out in the flats, past the muddy tulip fields, with swans watching them. They pick up Swinomish hitchhiker who has a mask. It has a charged life. Sits in the back with Pinocchio.

—12/ /15, 8 AM

They go to bookstore to get author's book. The owner doesn't have it, but Pinocchio shoplifts a book, *How to Draw the Female Nude*. They drive out to author's house.

—1/2/16

Round lake, deep without end. He takes Pinocchio
there and tosses him in.
                        —1/12/16, job

His face was painted with a grin. There was no reason
to find it sinister.
                        —1/20/15, job

Pinocchio knocks water valve with wrench—alley
starts to flood—Blue Fairy saves us.

Tic Toc sinks into mud.
"See you in eighty years!" Pinocchio crowed.

"One Adult, one Child."
"Child?"
                        —2/18/16

I take Pinocchio on drive at night in the Model T
truck. The fog is so thick we have to get out. Pinocchio sits on hood of truck as we roll along. I was so
mad at him, if we ran into something he would be the
first to go.
                        —2/19/16, job

I wrote *Pinocchio in America* in two large dollar store notebooks and I guess I forgot about the original blue notebook that had all these ideas. Anyway, they waited a long time to join the manuscript. The last message appears seventeen pages from the adventure's end and I'm surprised I didn't use it. It's from 5/17/16, 6:33 AM:

"One night the mermaid calls the radio station."

—A F
32nd Street, February 11, 2019

Pinocchio in America

"Yes, my friends," said Pinocchio, recovering his breath and with it his speech, "it is I, Pinocchio. I swam the ocean to be with you. I came to your land seeking fame and fortune and freedom."

Pinocchio in America
by Angelo Petri

He fell from the sky at noon that bright spring day, and the sea swallowed him up within just a few yards of the shore…Legends galore about his strange disappearance are circulated among the pilots who fly across the seas, and are the theme of daydreams and fairy-tales among the Italian children whom he loved so well. Some day a poet worthy of the task will write an epic about him.

My Air Armada
by Air Marshal Italo Balbo

CHAPTERS

I.
How It Happened That I Went Happily To Work

I began the day with a lie. I called in sick. I'm sure I'm not the only one do this.

"You're not sick!" my brother said.

"No, I am."

"Get in here!" This was coming from a guy who practically lives at work. Sometimes he won't leave the shop until after 7 PM. "If you can pick up the phone and call me, you can hop on your Wheel and get here."

You might have thought he had me on the ropes, there was no turning back, it was all over for me. But I worked up a cough and let it go.

"Get in here!" he repeated. "Don't make me come over there. I'll drag you to work by the collar!"

"My Wheel is broken." That was my last try.

"Take a cab then. I'm giving you thirty minutes." He hung up.

I loaded the phone back in the wall. It fit snugly against the spring mechanism. If he called me back in five minutes it would leap off the wall and find me. There was no escape.

Why couldn't I be sick? That's one of the problems working with family—they know you. Also, it's June. Who gets sick in June? I would have to wait until the winter to make it believable. Don't think I won't! I'll show my brother he can't do this to me. Maybe I'll be sick for two days.

It's not that I'm trying to get out of work—well, it is—it's just, aren't we there enough? Do we have to spend all of our brief life devoted to day after day, 8-5? Surely it's not wrong once in a while to feel what it must be like for a bird—to just go about the neighborhood pleasantly and do what you want to do. Yes, I, a human being, envy the birds! When I was a boy, one of my favorite things to do was stand on a fence and sing like a bird. There are people who make a living that way. Why can't I be one?

"Hey!" the wall telephone chirped.

"Yes?"

"You have twenty two minutes to get to work."

"Okay, okay!"

II.
Sneaking Past A Talking Lawnmower

There was nothing wrong with my Wheel. Well, it wasn't in perfect condition—it rattled and squeaked and the steering handle was loose—but I knew it would get me to work. It always did.

I opened the garage door. Sunlight slanted across the dark floor. The Wheel was waiting for me beside cans of paint, brooms and cobwebs.

The lawnmower rolled away from the wall, just enough to block my path. Its bladed mouth chattered, "Is it time to mow the lawn again?"

I hear voices. Just about everywhere I go I hear voices telling me what to do and how to behave. I can't even call in sick on my home telephone, or leave the garage without an argument. You can imagine the sort of trouble I have doing just about anything. I don't know if it's my conscience relaying itself to objects around me. I also talk to myself. As I'm talking to you. Aren't there voices everywhere? The whole planet is alive and telling us things—all you have to do is listen.

I told the lawnmower, "No, it's not time. Not now. I have to go to my job."

"Right…Your job…What do you do there anyway?"

"I've told you before. I work at the Auto Repair. I fix dents in cars. Also scratches, bends, all those things."

"Yeah, well don't forget about the lawn."

"I won't."

"What's it look like anyway?"

"It's fine."

"Looking a little shaggy?"

"No, it's fine. I promise I'll let you know when it needs mowing."

The mower pouted, "Seems like a while since I ran out there."

I sighed. I had to get to work and here I was stuck talking with a lawnmower. "Don't worry about it." I grabbed hold of the Wheel handle. "I have to go. Maybe when I get home tonight I'll take you out to the yard."

"Maybe, huh? I hate to get my hopes up…"

He could grumble and grouse all he wanted. "I have to go," I repeated. I was glad he didn't have the power to move any further from the wall. I'm sure my ankle made a tempting target. All he could do was wiggle his rusted stanchion and clack his blades. He was grumpy alright. All he needed was a cigar clamped in those steely blades. Maybe I would get him one at the 5 and Dime. One of the exploding kinds! That made me almost laugh.

I stopped the Wheel in the driveway and as I reached up to pull the garage door back down, I caught sight of the lawnmower. He had a long day before him, sitting in the dark, watching spiders and dust. I felt a little sorry for him as I said, "See you tonight."

I didn't expect him to answer. It was too bad he didn't have a cigar plugged in the corner of those blades. He could have chewed the end and glared.

III.
Meeting My Brothers On The Way To The Clay

Everyone was in a bad mood today. When I got to work and parked my Wheel, my brother was there before I even cut the motor.

"I was giving you two more minutes," he warned me.

The motor chittered and stopped. "Until what?" I asked. I guess I just wanted to see him get mad.

"Until I drove out to your crummy little hovel and beat down the door with my fists!" He held up his balled hands and shook them. I knew he wasn't exaggerating. Still, I couldn't help smiling. He looked like the Big Bad Wolf. "You're lucky I don't fire you!"

"I know." I stepped out of the Wheel. "I'm so lucky our father wanted all his sons to work together."

"Lucky…" He spat at the cracked asphalt and turned on his heel to go back to his office.

I guess I'm what you would call the blacksheep of the family. I've never been that interested in making good, climbing the job ladder and all the other trappings of the so-called American dream. I live in an alley, don't I?

I am lucky that when our father retired, he specified that his sons carry on the business and care for his houses (my brother got one) and other properties (the garage being mine). Really, he did leave me well cared for. I just have to work part-time at the auto repair, the sort of easy job anyone could do.

The office door slammed shut. My brother would probably gripe about me, tell the secretary how close he was to blowing my house down and then he'd pour himself some coffee and go to his desk.

Fortunately I have my job out back. I walked across the parking lot full of cars gleaming in the sun, around the corner of the garage. The sunflowers I planted along the wall don't have much stamina. Maybe I don't water them enough? Maybe it was a bad idea to begin with…I don't have much of a green thumb. I mostly use my hands on clay.

Behind the garage, out of sight of customers and partly camouflaged by blackberry is a solid bank of clay, fifteen feet tall. You might say that's my bread and butter. There were claw marks left in it from my shovel.

"Hi Toc!" I called out. Tic Toc works in the garage. The back door was rolled open and I could see him standing there. Tic Toc has worked here for years. He's quite a sight by now. Everyone gets older, feels the ravages of time in their back or knees, but every part of him has taken the toll. Not much of him is human anymore. He resembles a mechanical man, made of the most durable materials found laying around.

Toc held up a metal arm and tapped its wrist with a hand made out of flesh and two spoons. "You're late!"

He was more of a stickler for time than my other brother. His heavy right arm was encrusted with a big wall clock. He was always glancing at the face of it and sometimes he would stop whatever he was doing so he could wind it with a brass key kept looped around his neck. I guess that clock keeps him running too.

"I know…" I replied. "I'm not feeling too good today. I wanted to stay home but Bruno wouldn't let me."

"If you can walk, you can work."

I laughed. That was Tic Toc's rule. Of course if he couldn't walk, he would just tie on a new leg. You can't say it hasn't happened before.

There was one day he was so stressed he actually blew apart. Bruno and I had to sweep all his parts together and it took us the afternoon to put him back together.

Since then he's had a pressure valve installed to let off steam. It's not uncommon to find him bowed over some job, head in a vapor.

So, having been scolded, I walked to where my work begins every day, at the wall of clay.

IV.
The Story of Spig Levatt And His Baseball Bat

You can barely read the name anymore. When Spig Levatt showed up at the shop to have some chrome work done, everyone went crazy. Everybody wanted his autograph. Our secretary Arlis has a photograph of the two of them. You would have thought he was the King of Siam. So I got him to sign my shovel for me, right on the wooden handle, the way they do with baseball bats.

Sometimes in the late afternoon with the radio in the garage tuned to a baseball game, I will hear Spig Levatt take a swing at home plate, or make some spectacular catch way out in the field, with the crowd roaring like a wind machine.

V.
Showing The Milkman Around Town

I don't know how exciting it would be to describe my job. I won't bore you with the details of manufacture. I hope that my neglect doesn't cause what I do here to become one of those lost art forms like levitation. The procedure of turning clay into what resembles polished silver chrome just isn't that exciting. This isn't alchemy.

As long as the clay deposit holds out we can continue to work on cars. Maybe someday I'll dig the shovel in and hit nothing but gravel. Who knows? There's got to be an end eventually.

I used to be worried about finding something other than clay. Tic Toc told me about the guy working the wall before me. I didn't know the story until Bruno hired me. Toc really set the mood. It was raining, it stayed dark all day, miserable in other words. My predecessor had a different shovel than me—that's one good thing. He stuck the blade in the wall and gave it a good kick to dig it in. I know all about this motion: the first bite of the shovel and then the big lift full of clay into the wheelbarrow. You get so used to it you feel it in your sleep. The rain on his back, dropping off his jacket sleeves onto his hands. But the second he started to turn towards the wheelbarrow, he was pulled back. Something was holding on to that shovel.

It was even worse hearing Tic Toc tell the story. He only has one good eye and he was close enough I could smell the metal on his breath. "Holding onto the end of the shovel with all of its might was a bony white skeleton hand!" Tic Toc's glass eye stared over my shoulder, far away back in time.

That rainy dark day was a long time ago, but I often think of it when I work. It's a little scary to realize there's this whole unseen world behind the wall of clay. Who knows what's in there? But so far, all I've run into is clay.

I never did hear the rest of the story either. Tic Toc blew up only moments later and I never wanted to bring it up again.

I do wonder what happened though.

Even on a warm day like this, with the sun on my back, it makes me shiver.

I don't like to think about it, but when I do I imagine that poor guy with the shovel, petrified with fright, getting pulled into the clay wall. As his feet disappear into it, one tennis shoe falls off and remains behind. Oh, and maybe the shovel is spit back out onto the parking lot, chewed like a toothpick.

That's one scenario—not a pleasant one. I've also thought of another one. The guy with the shovel is stronger and he pulls the skeleton free from the clay. There's actually not anything ferocious about the skeleton. As he stands there, brushing off his bones, he explains that he used to be a milkman. A long time ago he got caught in a flashflood and was buried in clay. He's thankful to be back in the world, but he's worried he never got to finish his deliveries. He's got to go; there are streets he hasn't been to yet. He offers his cold white bony hand and it's like shaking a clutch of broken twigs.

I prefer the second version and I'm sticking to it.

The guy before me never met a talking skeleton before. He offered to show the milkman around town.

Things had changed during that long stay underground. He got the bone man an old pair of coveralls from the garage and they walked away from the clay, never to return again.

VI.
Time Running Like Water

It's not June anymore. Where has the time gone? I've been at work or home, going back and forth. Summer is over and it's the end of September. It's getting colder, the rainy days are on the way and Lynden Milan is in the alley, shutting off the water supply. He does that a lot. I think there was a problem with it at one time. Some long ago winter the pipes froze and he has devoted his life to preserving that by reliving it.

I stood there and watched him. I let him do it. When he's done I can open the valve again.

In fact he won't even notice what I've done. He won't say a word. Lynden Milan can only speak in the past tense.

He held his wrench and gave the spigot one last try. It was tight. He was satisfied. He would be thinking of a cold winter years ago, I guessed. Maybe this year will be another one, maybe he knows something I don't?

He straightened back up and followed the building along its south side, towards the fields. He had other jobs to do again.

I let him go without saying hello. It's okay though. I'll see him again I'm sure. Then you'll know what I mean. It can be strange talking with him. No stranger than talking with someone from a foreign land, which I suppose is what he is. We all have our ways of living in the world. Other people are probably just as confusing to him. I've seen him look right through some people, but I've been here long enough that he accepts me.

Caught in routine, he went back around the garage. Maybe there were more water lines to turn off. Maybe he was walking with someone he used to know, someone invisible to me.

It's easy to let the days just rush away from you. It's a comfort to have someplace like the alley where time is sealed.

VII.
At Home In The Last Century

We live in an old town where the 20th Century still survives. I like it. I'm surrounded by the last century. I don't know if there's ever been a simpler age, but I like the way these old things rest in time. They have a sort of nobility and graceful quality. They carried us to where we are today. Their work is over and they rest, still carrying a glow. I've been stuck in the last century for years. Time moves slower in an alley. Like a slough broken off from a river, there are things happening now that won't even reach here.

The old America, the time of my grandfather and grandmother, is fading away. I guess that's what this country is, layers of its past. That's why I chose to live where that past I like streams and pools into this narrow alley like a tide.

You wouldn't believe the things I surround myself with.

I don't even know what a lot of it is. Sometimes I just stack them in piles.

Other things I've been able to revive and put to use again.

In the evening, once the stars start to appear, I go to the radio station.

VIII.
The Discovery Of The Radio Station

I do a lot of exploring in the alley. Things pour in here and take refuge, getting stranded like driftwood on a beach. I don't know if the wind brings them here or if it's some magnetic force, but this is a landscape that's always changing with the addition of new old things.

One day an iron fire escape attached itself to a brick wall. It looked like it had always been there, rusted to the bricks. Being a curious person, I accepted its invitation and followed the steps to the roof. I don't often get a view above the alley. There's a telephone pole I like to climb, but usually I keep to the ground, or if indoors, no more than the second or third floor.

When I stepped off the stairway I was met by another new sight. Planted on the rooftop was a sort of miniature Eiffel Tower, an intricately made radio antenna with the call letters KGUS bolted to it.

I was impressed. Fifty feet up, at the very top of it, was a red beacon. No doubt that would shine in the night. I walked around the base of it admiring the workmanship and design. It also looked like something a dirigible might anchor to. In the shadow of it was a plain looking wooden kiosk the size of a telephone booth. The door had the black letters KGUS painted on it. I wasn't surprised to find it unlocked.

That's how I discovered the radio station, left exactly as it had been in 1957. There were posters and records on the wall, pictures of the unbelievable people who used to play rock n roll.

IX.
The Hidden River Below The Alley

It didn't take me long to try out the radio station. I found the power switch. In a moment the yellow dials glowed and the needles jumped. The record player began to spin, gaining speed. One of them held an LP and the sound of it wound, crackled and yawned into life.

Now I climb the fire escape just about every night and follow the roof to the stairs leading down into KGUS. My radio show flies out of there like an owl.

Where does the music I play go? Is there anyone out there listening? I don't know I haven't heard. I just let the airwaves carry it over roofs and fields and trees and roads and finally to the stars, I suppose.

I play a lot of torch songs. They appeared on the shelf as if they had grown there, the fruit of some tree we don't see the likes of anymore. They used to stand someone in front of a full orchestra and let them pour their hearts out. You would have thought love was the only thing worth living for and the way those songs carried on one after the other like a blue stream, you would have believed it too. I know I do.

After the last song ended and the needle bumped and scratched at the record's center, I turned the station off.

The room was quiet. I don't usually think about love anymore, I guess I'm used to being alone. But tonight I felt like the only person left in the world.

I found my way out of the dark studio, but instead of going back up onto the roof, I followed my lantern down the hallway. There's no telling what you might find in these old buildings. Once I found an entire wax museum. They were all there—all the forgotten famous people standing around waiting to be noticed again. I'll admit I considered bringing them into the alley and lining them up like streetlamps. I wondered if I could turn them into candles, so their slow burning light could shine the way.

My lantern glowed on a door at the end of the hall.

When I turned the handle, there was a staircase pouring down into what I supposed was the basement. I followed the steps. Why not? All those songs still haunted me and I felt like I didn't have much to lose. I've never find anything really that bad around here, just some ghosts sometimes.

The stairs came to rest on a concrete floor. It leveled out for about thirty square feet, a gloomy empty room with a black window that reflected back the bright glare of my lantern.

I shut my eyes and doused the wick and the light was gone. My sight adjusted to the quiet dark. After a minute, I could actually see the window. It was like a gray-blue TV screen. It held just enough dim moonlight to reveal slivery shadows moving past.

I walked forward towards the window until I could put my hands upon the glass. Like submarines, ghostly salmon swam past. Below the alley I live on was a hidden river. Some of the big fish looked right back at me. Their mouths moved as if they were talking some language I could see, but couldn't know.

X.
The Blue Fairy Appears, But I Don't Know It Yet.

I thought of those fish as I walked along the alley cobblestones back home. They were below me, twenty feet or so, in that subterranean blue current. I wondered who put that window there…someone who liked to watch fish apparently.

There was a cool breeze in the alley. It was autumn and a few leaves were stirred by the wind. They may have crawled here like the other things. Maybe they were from some older time too, survivors off a tree that had been knocked down to make a shopping mall or a parking lot.

My house was waiting for me.

Those torch songs stayed with me. They walked with me. It was hard to shake their feeling. I was surrounded by memories and the past.

A blue light reflected in my window. It moved on the glass. It was only there for a second or so, then gone.

If we had fireflies, I would have guessed that's what it was, but we don't and I don't know what could have made such a small flying blue light. It made me wonder.

I didn't see anything strange about my house. The night painted it black. I went around the corner towards the backyard. The grass behind the garage was long—I knew the lawnmower would have something to say about that. The moonlight showed the grass was tall enough to hide your shoes.

Stars shined. An airplane slid across the sky

towards the city. That blue dot of light could have disappeared up there. Endless worlds floated in space. I didn't know it then but I would see that light again.

XI.
What Gathers In The Airwaves At Night

Even after all my time in the alley, there are still things I haven't found, mysteries and archaeology I haven't discovered. For instance (like an elephant hidden in my midst) there's a TV station broadcasting from somewhere nearby. It seems like it would be in that same building as the radio station, sharing the same antenna. Who knows? There are other doors I haven't tried. Maybe those salmon in the basement are surrounding an underwater studio tethered by cables to KGUS? Television signals nest among the bricks in the day and fly about the alley at night. I'm glad for the company.

Before I fall asleep, I like to fill the screen of my wooden TV. Usually it's some black and white comedy, or an adventure on the road that follows the dream logic of another America. As I watched the end of one movie, a villain was chased through a foggy city. Of course they finally caught him, shot him off a rooftop and then it was the end, the woman and man who survived in the swirling shapes of cloud. I turned the TV off and crawled into bed. My window was open some and I could hear a trumpet playing in the cold night.

Even though I'm surrounded by an alley full of old things and ghosts, I'm not the only living citizen. Cornelius Barter has been staying in an apartment a couple blocks away. I don't know much about him. I've only seen him a few times. He's not much for words. It seems he came here to get away from the world, to drop out of sight.

The sound of his trumpet says it all. It sounds wounded and sadder than words.

I lay there and listened. I could also hear the breeze. After a little while the sound of him was gathered into that wind and drawn away down the alley off to the distant dark sleeping fields outside of town. Farewell, Cornelius Barter.

It's a relatively easy life for me, I have to admit. I go to work, I come home. When I get home, I do the things I like to do. Of course they say when you think you've got it easy and all figured out, that's when things change. In my case they did. Little did I know what the next day had in store.

XII.
I Make A Wish

There was nothing unusual about the start of the day. Who would have thought my adventures were about to begin by sneaking past a talking lawnmower? How could I know my old world was about to disappear?

I was quiet and the lawnmower didn't notice me. Now that summer was gone there was no reason for him to be awake. He would stay asleep until some sunny day in the spring. A rusty eye will open then.

I didn't disturb him as I pushed the velocipede out the door. It was cold outside, my breath stuck in the air.

I got the Wheel started and we were on our way. At the end of the alley, I took a right. I waited for traffic to let me in. There weren't any cobblestones, the road was poured smooth and the big wheel hissed on the wet surface. It must have rained during the night.

The buildings towered on either side of me. I haven't said much about the world outside of the alley. Have you seen pictures of those alpine villages with carved, leaning wooden walls and window boxes…or those old side streets in Brooklyn strung with clotheslines? All the bright colors of a town seen in Rishikesh…

Well it's not like any of that. Nowadays the buildings are poured out of plastic moulds. About half a mile from the alley, I took another right onto Magnolia. I passed a mile of gray colored architecture and rolled into the parking lot of Geppetto Auto Repair.

I scooted past the parking lot, cut the motor and glided to my usual spot. I got out before the big wheel toppled.

Tic Toc stood in the garage glazing a maroon fender. I had the whole day to small talk. The radio was on, with an annoying jingle they like to replay. The red dust of clay sugared across the gray cement and gravel as I walked automatically towards my place at the wall. Just once, I thought, I'd like to see something different.

Maybe I shouldn't have made that wish.

How was I to know that up through all those clouds, above the world like a rocket past our atmosphere and moon, outside our orbit, beyond all the planets we know, a tiny glint of a star had just granted me my wish.

My shovel waited for me in the wheelbarrow. Neither one of us really wanted to work this morning. Luckily, I would only need it a little while.

XIII.
The Voice Calling From The Ground

At first I thought I struck a root. There are some big trees growing up beyond the wall and sometimes they send shoots like veins through the clay. I gripped the shovel tighter and pulled it free. I would have to give it some muscle to cut through the root. I would have, if I didn't hear at that very moment the sound of a muffled cry. It sounded like someone trapped in a suitcase, or Houdini locked in his underwater safe. I looked around myself.

Toc was in the garage, his back to me. The radio was jingling. It was business as usual, only it wasn't.

I heard the voice again and this time I could tell where it was coming from. Something was calling me from the clay.

As I chipped away at the sediment, I wondered what it could be. I took my time and was careful. It couldn't be anything alive under all that crushing weight of earth—maybe it was a time capsule with a recording that my shovel set off. There was a story in one of my old Sci-Fi pulps about a man who found a door buried in the ground. When he opened it, he saw stairs leading to a whole other world, hollowed underground. I also thought of another possibility. Maybe it was just an old telephone buried in a mudslide…The operator had been holding on diligently for the call to go through.

What I thought was a root, the smooth section of wood my shovel had nicked, revealed itself in the clay. There was fabric attached to it, soiled red and green cloth. By now the sound of the voice was persistent, rattling on like a radio from the next room.

I brushed clay off a small wooden arm. The hand clenched into a tight fist. I wasn't afraid. It was a doll. Didn't they make them with a string you could pull, then a spinning little disc inside would play words? This one must be stuck. I cleared the soil from its balled fingers and that's when the hand opened and seized me.

I didn't know if it was a spring mechanism designed to do that, but it was such a surprise I gave a yell. It still clung tightly to my fingers.

I used my free hand to claw at the layer of clay around the doll's body. More and more of it began to appear. It wore red shorts and its leg tapered into a sharp black shoe. All the while the mechanism within it yammered away unintelligibly like a buzzing beehive.

And I still couldn't get the wooden hand to let go of me! Half its body was in the daylight as I removed the clay around its face. It seemed to be a wooden boy doll. He wore a red pointed cap on his black painted hair. I took a quick look over my shoulder to see if Tic Toc was watching, but he was busy in the garage. Nobody had seen what I found. Nobody had seen what had found me, I mean. I could imagine what my brother would say if he saw me standing by the clay wall holding a half-buried doll. Wouldn't he just love that!

I turned my attention back to that doll when the pressure on my hand eased. A trickle of soil fell in my sleeve as the wooden grip let go of me, as the clay around it bowed and the arm popped free. I stared, mesmerized. I was beginning to think the doll had a life of its own.

And even as the doll moved slightly in the clay like someone stirring under blankets, I stayed frozen, watching. Part of me refused to believe this was really happening.

The head turned from its profile position and popped free to stare at me. Those painted eyes must have seen nothing but dark for ages and they focused on me like coals. Its wooden mouth opened and it coughed. It took a deep breath, as any living thing would do, and then spoke, "What took you so long?"

XIV.
Pinocchio Hops And Dances And Runs Away

A bird was chirping from some unseen tree way above. I could also hear the radio in the garage. Toc was tapping something with a hammer. These were the everyday sounds I've grown used to. They made sense.

The thing in the clay struggled and spilled a clot of soil onto my shoes. That slender arm reached towards me. "Do you think you could give me a hand out of here?" It had already taken hold of the thick cloth of my coat. There wasn't much choice. It didn't take much effort for the puppet to leave the clay wall. My still uncomprehending mind told me it was a puppet, not a lifeless doll—the limbs were segmented and moved as if they were being pulled by strings I just couldn't see them. Maybe there was a circus in town? Maybe they were doing stunts like this all over town?

"Okay," the puppet said. "You can set me down now. I'm not Mary Pickford." He squirmed in my arms. I say 'he' because the voice was a boy's, and he seemed to be alive as a real boy.

When I leaned over, the moment his feet touched the ground he let out a hoot and jumped in a circle. He threw his arms around like a boy swatting bees.

It was about this moment I found my voice. I know it sounds like a crazy thing to say but I was afraid I recognized him. "Are you Pinocchio?"

He stopped hopping about, landing on one foot, then slowly lowering the other. I still couldn't see any strings pulling him.

Pinocchio stared at me, "You've heard of me?"

"Of course. Your book is pretty well known. They even made movies about you."

"That doesn't surprise me. I was famous before I got thrown out of an airplane. I imagine people have been missing me..." He pivoted and stopped when he saw what was in the garage. Tic Toc looked like a robot as he toiled, making inferior car parts out of clay. "I must have been underground for a long time! What year is it?"

"2015."

Pinocchio shook his head, "What's 2015 minus 1933?"

"I don't know." I pictured the numbers written on a chalkboard. I was never good at math.

"I bet that robot knows," Pinocchio said and before I could stop him, he sprang from me and was on his way to the car garage. I ran after him, but he had a head start.

XV.
Tic Toc Has The Best Day Of His Life

Pinocchio was fast. He scurried over to the table and leaped up in front of Toc.

My brother dropped the bright chrome gas cap and it shattered like a diamond.

"How are you at numbers?" Pinocchio said. I got there as he asked my dumbfounded brother, "What's 2015 minus 1933?"

I panted, "Tic Toc…" and he held his metal glove up to hush me.

"82," he answered.

"I was stuck in that clay for eighty two years!"

"You're Pinocchio!" Tic Toc steamed.

Pinocchio gave a cockeyed grin and said, "This mechanical man is a genius!"

Tic Toc laughed. I couldn't believe it. I don't think I've ever seen him laugh before. Then he gave Pinocchio a big rough hug. Another first. He told Pinocchio, "Your book was my favorite when I was a kid." That was news to me. Tic Toc picked him up and gave him another hug. "It's good to see you again."

"Easy!" Pinocchio wheezed. "You can set me down."

"Oh yeah, of course," Toc said.

"You got a name?"

"Tic Toc Geppetto."

"Thanks, Tic Toc. How did you ever manage without me?"

Tic Toc laughed again. "This is what I've been doing. Actually it's sort of because of you. I like building things. When I was a kid I made a robot of you."

"Hah!" Pinocchio laughed. "And now you work on carriages."

"Where you been all these years anyway?" Tic Toc asked.

I was actually speechless watching this conversation. It was like watching a play.

Pinocchio made himself rigid with his arms at his side. He muttered out the corner of his mouth. "I was buried alive. Held pressed tight beneath the layers of that clay over there." Then his wiry body sprang to life. "Eighty two years later and Pinocchio has returned!" He raised his thin arms over his head and shook them like a boxer.

"Good to have you back," said Tic Toc. He reached out and clasped Pinocchio's hand. Toc seemed to have lost his mind. Maybe there was someone else under all that tin? Anyway, he was having the best day of his life at Geppetto Auto Repair. "Hey! You gotta meet the boss."

Pinocchio grinned. "Certainly!"

It was lunacy. I stood there and watched Pinocchio hop off the work table and follow Toc through the garage to the door that led to the office.

XVI.
Geppetto Auto Repair Finds A Spokesman

I hurried after them. I seemed to remember in his book he would do this all the time—he would just take off running whenever he wanted to. This was another one of those adventures.

They were already to the door when I caught up and as Toc opened it, I heard my brother Bruno give a shout. I could tell this was going to go badly.

But once again, I was wrong. My brothers were spellbound by Pinocchio. In no time he was dancing around them and they were roaring with laughter. It didn't seem right to me. Was I wrong to feel a little distrustful of that marionette?

"Look!" my brother yelled. "It's Pinocchio!"

"I know," I replied.

Pinocchio pointed at me, "He saved me! I was fossilized in that cliff for eighty two years!"

"Hey!" Bruno told me, "Good job."

Arlis cooed, "He's adorable!"

Pinocchio bowed. It made me remember the old cartoon he was in. He was in a puppet show. Didn't he fall off the stage for a laugh?

Bruno leaned in close to the marionette and asked, "Can you do that thing when you tell a lie?"

"It doesn't happen anymore!" Pinocchio said. If possible, he beamed. "After eighty two years in a rock you learn self-control. I'm fine if I lie, nobody can tell. Look," he raised his voice, "This is the greatest place I've ever been in my life!"

Nothing happened.

Bruno clapped his hands suddenly. "Hey! I got an idea. Pinocchio, you gave me an idea!"

"Hold on," Arlis said, "Let me write this down."

Bruno waited while she got a notepad and a pen off her desk. He waited with a finger held in the air like one of those old Roman statues.

"Okay," she said. "Shoot."

Bruno took a deep breath and roared, "We put Pinocchio in a commercial!"

Pinocchio hopped and Toc nodded like a piston had tripped in his head. Everyone was over the moon.

"I'll get Pop on the phone," Arlis told us.

"Can't you see it?" I heard Bruno crow. I wasn't looking though. I stared out the window at the cliff. My shovel lay out there by the scene of the crime.

XVII.
Pinocchio Is A Star, But Did Anyone Else Even Read His Book?

Things were moving fast now. Bruno drove us. We sat spread along the front seat. I was in the middle holding Pinocchio. He was pointing out sights like a time traveler, the futuristic new world he had never seen before.

Imagine that—a whole new world. Everything was a miracle.

Even before we made it out the office door to the parking lot, Pinocchio halted at the snack machine. He got my brothers to spend eight dollars on it. He stood with his hands on the glass like someone at an aquarium, fascinated as the wire moved aside and let another candy bar fall into a tray below. By the time we pried him from there he held a tight bundle of sweets clutched in his arms.

Bruno and Tock got a kick out of Pinocchio's reaction. As we drove along the bay, he kicked from me and crawled over Bruno's lap to stick his head out the window like a dog. He chattered in Italian. A woman on the curb stared at him.

By the time we got to our father's house, I knew it was far too late to return the marionette to clay. You can't close Pandora's Box. Pinocchio sprang out the door with Bruno and Tock each holding a wooden hand. They lifted him off the ground between them as he kicked his spindly legs wildly. It was already the scene from a commercial, a happy family on a crisp sunny winter day—all it needed was soft focus and music. The trees were lively with birds as we crossed the lawn. All that was missing was the warm baritone of the announcer, "Geppetto Auto Repairs Cares." Pinocchio was a star.

And it was the same story when my father met the puppet.

"He can't lie!" Bruno said. "So when he says we're the best car repair, people will know it's the truth, otherwise his nose would grow."

"That's right," Pinocchio agreed.

"Well, I think he's great," said our father. "You have Arlis fill out the paperwork. Let's get this on film."

My brothers clapped hands and cried out. Pinocchio clattered about the living room manically.

Why was I the only one who had doubts? Was I the only one who remembered his book?

XVIII.
I Decide Not To Work The Rest Of The Day

When we got back to the garage, half the day had drifted by. I left them in the office and walked all alone back to the wall of clay. I planned on doing a little bit of work, believe it or not. But I didn't. I stared at that cavity Pinocchio dropped out of and I just didn't feel like working. My shovel didn't mind. It leaned against the wall of clay like someone waiting for a trolley.

Besides, what else might be waiting for me in that clay? A wooly mammoth? A car full of gangsters from 1924? Until now, I never thought my job could be so unpredictable.

As I stood there digressing, it began to rain. I just noticed it. Little sparks of rain on my hands and face.

It was Pinocchio's influence that made me turn away from the clay and the garage and find my Wheel and leave. He wasn't the only one to follow his heart.

XIX.
Crossing Paths With A Bat

A fine spray hissed around me as I turned from the street, back to my alley. I was never so glad to see the gables of the old buildings. Dusk was falling and everything looked like a black and white movie before me.

What a crazy day it had been! I stopped in front of the garage door. Where was the world I left only hours before? Little did I know how rare my life had been, and what changes a day at the clay would bring.

I opened the big wooden door and pushed the velocipede right past the lawnmower with nary a word. A gray February night was beginning. The lawnmower was far away with his thoughts, dreaming of blue and green summer days when the lawn would grow an inch in the sun.

I crept back to the door and shut it behind me. Then I just stood there for a while and looked at the alley. A bat went toppling through the air clumsily, going out to another night. I've seen him before. He often returns in the dawn when I start out for work. Our paths only cross when one of us is coming home and the other is going out. He flies like a crumpled piece of paper. I don't know how he stays in the sky, from gutters and eaves to the breeze around the steeple.

He disappeared into silhouettes.

I listened to the sound of dripping water. I looked at the gray thick layer of clouds pulled overhead. I thought of them as stitched together and holding up a wide deep lake. The wind jostled and spilled it and sometimes the seams would tear. Didn't Pinocchio tell me he fell out of the sky? I thought of him up there in a balloon basket, falling overboard. Down, down, down, right into a deep hole in the ground. The years passed. Rain drops rattled on a trash can lid.

XX.
Pinocchio Finds Me, Then Finds Something Better

I made spaghetti. I was washing the dishes and the cooking pan when there was a knock at the door. I wasn't expecting anyone, I never am. I couldn't remember the last time someone visited. Walking toward the sound, I remembered once my brother showed up, banging on the door to wake me up for work. But this insistent knock was more like a bird tapping, a woodpecker hanging on the latch.

There didn't seem to be anyone out there in the black night as I turned the handle and let in the cool air. Suddenly my knees almost buckled as Pinocchio leaped inside and tackled me.

"Did you miss me?!" he cried out.

Missing is one of those colossal conditions the torch singers know so well. A haiku poet can circle it, and capture it in just a few powerful words. With Pinocchio I would come to experience a whole new world of missing.

His grip was tight as a clothespin on me and then he let go. "Guess what?" He clapped his hands together sharply. "Tomorrow I get to be in a movie!"

"Oh," I said.

"I'm so excited!" He skipped around the room.

I said, "The commercial?"

"Yes!" He hopped onto a chair and froze on it with his arms outstretched. "I can't wait for tomorrow!"

"Are my brothers here too?" I peered into the dark alley.

"No. They dropped me off. They'll be ready for me

when it's bright and early in the morning."

"Why did they bring you here though?"

"They said I needed some rest for my big day tomorrow." He threw himself off the chair with his arms held like wings. For a moment I expected him to fly. But he landed on the floor beside the old Philco radio. His head tipped and turned in a full revolution. "You know what?" he said after he'd seen the whole room. "This place looks just like my father's house back in Italy." He strolled lazily, hands in pockets. "That clock, that painting, that bookshelf, that bed, that woodstove, that teapot, that window, that broomstick."

What was I going to do with him? How could I wind him down?

"Everything in one room," he continued. "You should see Bruno's house. It's a palace compared to this." He stopped by the window and stared. "Does this open?" he said and before I could speak, he stood on his tiptoes and gave it a push.

It was a bit of a cool night and all these doors and windows opening made a draft in the room.

"What's this?" Pinocchio said, tipping his head. "I hear something!"

The sound of a frail trumpet floated in the breeze.

"What is that?" Pinocchio cupped a hand like a wooden shell to his ear.

"My neighbor," I said. "He's a jazz musician."

"*Jazz!*" Pinocchio's head popped and swiveled towards me. "You mean like Louis Armstrong? Bix Beiderbecke? Lester Young? Chick Webb? Harry Sweets Edison?!"

"Right...I guess so."

"Who's your neighbor?"

"Cornelius Barter."

Pinocchio listened. I recognized the song, it was one of those old standards I play on my radio show.

Suddenly Pinocchio shot over the window ledge and disappeared from sight. I heard the clack as he hit the cement outside and his footsteps as he got up and ran.

Can I be honest? I wasn't displeased to see him go. I was looking forward to my radio show alone. Can you imagine what Pinocchio would do in that small studio room filled with records and a microphone? So I let him go.

By the time I was done with the dishes, the night had settled down on the alley. As I walked to KGUS, the only sound was me.

XXI.
Alone After Radio

And the only sound coming home was the wind that had picked up, rattling the branches of the TV aerials, pouring over the cobblestones like a creek. I did look in the direction of Cornelius Barter's apartment. Sometimes a light shines in that window. But not tonight.

No sign of Pinocchio in my room either. The clock ticked. The panes on the alley side rattled with each gust. The timbers of my little house groaned. I didn't know where Pinocchio was. I was so tired I went straight to bed.

XXII.
A Note From Pinocchio

It wasn't the sleep I hoped for though. An endless-seeming Pinocchio movie played until dawn. A series of misadventures paraded. I forgot all the details as soon as I rolled out of bed; it was a vague melted cartoon adventure.

Another day at work was awaiting me so I stumbled towards the sink to get water for tea. That's when I saw the note on the table.

I am going on tour
with Cornelius Barter

He didn't sign it, but he didn't need to.

I got dressed, I had breakfast, and before I left I stuffed the note in my pocket. I knew my brothers would be interested in this development.

XXIII.
I Tell The Truth And Bruno Sends Me To The Pit

A bright yellow truck was parked in the lot. As I turned past it to the back of the building, I read the blazing letters painted across the siding: Star Material Enterprises. I remembered they wanted to film their commercial today.

I was barely out of the hoop of my Wheel when Bruno's voice barked at me, "Where's Pinocchio?!" The office door banged behind him. Tic Toc and my father were with him. This wasn't going to be easy. They gathered around me before I knew what I was going to say.

Maybe Pinocchio can lie, but I knew I had to tell them the truth. I took out the crumpled note and handed it to Bruno.

As he stared at it, eyes widening, I was thrown right back to childhood. I've seen that look often, usually just before he tossed me down a hill or pushed me in a lake. He was furious, "What's this mean?!"

"What is it?" my father asked.

Toc clanked closer, an eye telescoping.

"He's gone," I told them.

"He can't be!" Bruno was livid. The note was crushed tight in his fist. If it was coal it would be a diamond.

"What happened?" my father said, "Where did he go?"

I explained, "He heard music last night—there's a jazz musician who lives near me. Pinocchio went crazy. He jumped out the window and ran off with him."

"And you didn't go after him?!" Bruno seethed.

"I can't catch him! He's a maniac! You've seen how he can leap around."

My father swept his hands out dramatically, "You *lost* Pinocchio!"

And that's when Arlis came around the corner from the front of the building. With her was a teenaged girl, cradling a film camera. They hadn't missed much of the commotion though. Arlis asked me, "Pinocchio's not here?"

"Yeah!" Bruno said. "And so how are we supposed to make a commercial without him?"

"We can shoot around him," said the girl with the camera. "I can get some footage of cars and the garage. We can film Pinocchio later, when you find him."

Bruno shook his head dismally and glared at the ground like a bull. I would hate to be that ground.

"It's okay," the girl promised, "There's enough here to get started."

"Sure," Tic Toc said. "Let's all get started." He put a metal hand on my brother's shoulder.

Bruno wore an outrageous three piece suit I had seen on him only once before, when our cousin was married. He heard the girl, but he looked at me. I had let him down. "Not you!" he told me. "You're going to the pit."

XXIV.
The Blue Fairy Comes To My Rescue

The pit was exactly what you would expect. I had a lantern, a shovel and a rope ladder connecting me to the outside world. That world was nothing but a tiny dot of light so small you could set it with a diamond on a wedding ring.

I've been in the pit before. It doesn't take much for Bruno to send me here…If I was daydreaming, or happened to laugh when he was near…There's a long list.

This place used to be a wishing well. The coins at my feet are old as dull colored as stones with all their wishes worn off. I don't know where all the water went either.

I took my time filling a bucket with money. It wouldn't have been hard to fill it up in a minute, but I weakly scraped the shovel across the layers and ladled some in. I guess I don't really mind being down here. I was all alone, and the outside world was a shiny dot of starlight far away.

Actually—I let the shovel slide from my hands—there were two points of light up there. How could that be? The rope ladder climbed towards the little gray blur of earthly sunshine, but beside it, and moving and getting bigger, a blue glow descended.

No longer a firefly, I could see form to it, the shape of a body, a woman wearing a dress that flowered around her like a blue flame.

Of course I had seen her before. And I thought she was only fiction! I made room for her to land on the piles of coins and as she did, the bright light of her softened. She stood just as tall as me and smiled.

"Are you the Blue Fairy?" I said. But that was so obvious I quickly added, "If you're looking for Pinocchio, I'm sorry. He's not here."

"That's right," she said. I know people say these things, but her voice was like a song. "I came here to find you."

"Me?"

"Pinocchio is in danger. He needs your help."

"*My* help? Oh no, I'm not so sure what I can do. I've never gone on any adventures, Blue Fairy. You should ask my brother Bruno."

She shook her head, "He wouldn't even be able to see me. It has to be you." And when she smiled at me and said, "I know you can do it," all of a sudden I knew I could.

I stood there and watched her rise back into the air. I saw her become a little blue star that merged with the dot of day. With her gone, I never felt so cold and alone. She left like the last spark of fire up a chimney.

XXV.
Thinking Of Her, I Make My Way Back Into The World

I thought about her—after I filled the bucket with a few hurried shovelfuls, and while I climbed that unsteady rope ladder rung by rung—and the more I thought of her, the more I wanted to see her again. Wasn't Pinocchio the same way? Didn't he fall at her feet and cry when she had to leave? I don't know what it is about her. Well, of course…isn't it obvious? She's magic! She's the Blue Fairy!

Maybe thinking about her made me lighter. I barely noticed the weight of the bucket, the lantern and the shovel. The light of the outside world got brighter until it poured on the brick lining of the well and I could hear the clinking hammer blows coming from the garage.

XXVI.
Botticelli Books

When I told Bruno I was leaving work to get Pinocchio back, I thought he was going to force me right back into the pit, but my father, Toc and Arlis, and the girl with the camera all said that was a good idea. In the end, he even gave me travel money, enough for a bus ticket, and I was on my way.

I left my Wheel at work and followed the street downtown. This would be my first trip out of town and I felt nervous. I patted my coat pocket where I had my money and the Cornelius Barter tour schedule that Arlis printed for me. That's all I was bringing with me. No change of clothes in a cardboard suitcase, no provisions, nothing else. I was going there to get Pinocchio and return home on the next bus. Hopefully nothing more was needed.

Something did occur to me a couple blocks from the station. I passed a door, I glanced at the display window, the row of books propped about and then I stopped and returned to Botticelli Books.

There was no way I could walk past that bright orange book.

I entered the shop and hurried to the window. The cover stared out at the street, the face on it laughing at his reflection. I reached over and fished it from the display. It was an old pulp hardbound with covers soft and worn, the pages yellowed. It was like holding the weight of a bird.

That was him on the cover alright. He hadn't changed a bit.

I opened the book and read *The Adventures of*

Pinocchio, 1931. Didn't Pinocchio tell me he got stuck in the clay in 1933? I still had to get that story from him. Well, we would have time to talk on the bus ride home.

I carried the book to the register. There were a couple other people standing between shelves. Music played, the kind that reminds you of walking in a forest.

At the counter, I passed the book to a girl with pond water eyes. When I was younger, I would have been a fool for her. I would have bought her flowers and songs and poured out my heart. It must have been the Blue Fairy who had me thinking that way.

She said, "I like this book too," and I knew that voice. As I stared, her eyes turned blue and for just that moment I knew who she was.

XXVII.
Filled With Thoughts On The Bus Between Towns

The Blue Fairy gave me the book. I acted like some sort of fool. I didn't know what to say. By the time I got to the bus station, I wasn't even sure I could believe what happened.

Buying a round trip ticket left me with only a handful of coins.

The bus was boarding. I hurried up and it grumbled like a dragon. I found a seat by the window and we were soon on the way.

This was my first time leaving town. I've never been on a bus before, or train, or an airplane. If not for this emergency, why would I need to go anywhere? I had the alley and all the world I needed there. I looked for it, a glimpse between the cement walls. There were cars and Wheels and traffic signs, fire-escapes, sentry boxes surrounded by sandbags.

Once I drove my Wheel out this way. There used to be a girl and—oh well—I know this will sound like a lie, but with her gone, I wanted to join the circus.

I saw an ad in the paper. I went to a brick building, up an old wooden stairway to the third floor. I didn't do well on the interview though. I tried a few different jobs before I settled at the auto repair.

When I got out of school, I got an office job. I found it so stressful I would wake up in the middle of the night and I couldn't fall back asleep thinking of things I didn't finish. It dawned on me this was not the way to live a life; this stress that didn't make any sense was a waste. So I took the job with my brothers. The work is simple. I earn enough to survive. I go home happy to do what I like to do.

I know there are people who do this day after day—they get to the end and say what was it all for? I'm lucky. I have something I love. I get to spin records at night.

I think of playing records as my real job. I don't know if anyone's listening. I don't even know if the airwaves carry out this far, but I don't care.

The bus ride gave me time to think about the life I was leaving. I was miles away. What if I never went back? With the road climbing up the mountain, I got a good look at the city below, off in the distance, the tall buildings caught in a hazy cloud.

XXVIII.
The Bird Taxi

It was evening when the bus pulled into town and I finally walked outside again. The air was a lot colder. I wished I had a better coat.

All I carried was the Pinocchio book. I didn't know where The Broken Gate was. That's the club where Cornelius Barter would be playing. I didn't have a lot of time to find it before the show. I looked both ways, up and down Main Street, hoping I would see it.

One thing I liked right away about this town— they still have cable cars!

Well…one anyway. It looked like a pale blue robin's egg, big enough to carry two people. Leaning against a telephone pole, a cable ran up to a string of shiny line that paralleled the ground about ten feet off the street. A short man stood next to it. He smoked a cigarette and gave me the carny eye. "Hey!" he called.

I walked towards him. What else was I going to do?

"I saw you get off the bus," he said, "You lost?"

He looked like he knew the town. He wore a yellow and black uniform with a visored hat that said Bird Taxi above the brim.

"I need to get to The Broken Gate."

He nodded. He removed what remained of his cigarette and dropped it on the sidewalk. "I can take you there."

"I was hoping you could give me directions. I don't have much money for the fare." I dug in my pocket and showed him a handful of change.

"Don't worry about it," he said. "Business is slow.

I'll take you by the Gate." He opened the little door on the gondola. It looked like a ride at an amusement park.

Why not? I got inside and it tipped up as I sat on the white plastic seat. He got in and sat on the seat opposite me. There wasn't much room for our legs in between.

"Okay," he said and he reached through the window to pull a rope.

We arose like a balloon. There was no glass on the windows. I held the edges as we rocked and went up.

"Yeah," he continued, "Business is slow tonight. I thought there'd be more than just you getting off the bus. At least someone with money…No offence."

The gondola gave a jolt as it reached its full height. The driver flipped a lever and set us in motion, ten feet above the curb.

I shielded my eyes as we drifted by a sodium streetlamp. The bright orange glow filled my head like a jack o' lantern. I opened my eyes when a moth landed on my finger. I shook it off.

It was weird looking out the window. We drifted at rowboat speed. "Bird taxi," I said.

We passed another telephone pole, and the flywheel, windlass, cogs and winches clicked as the cable fed through.

"How far is it to The Broken Gate?" I didn't see any sign of it among the clustered neon signs ahead.

"Look," he said.

The fact is, I could have walked there and I wouldn't have got stuck in a tree either.

The Bird Taxi driver shook the big limb that held us. The branches rattled and clattered. Our cable wire was tangled everywhere. Finally, he told me, "You might as well climb down."

"Climb down the tree?"

He ignored me though, reaching under his plastic seat, removing a bundle of rope. He pushed it to the door, turned the handle open and then he gave the bundle a kick.

A ladder unrolled out the doorway and hit the sidewalk.

I must have looked doubtful.

"Go ahead," he said. "You'll be fine. This happens all the time."

"Sorry about the tree."

"No, it's okay." He leaned out the window and shook the line. "I'll unsnag it eventually."

I slipped my book inside my raincoat so I could use both hands climbing.

Another ladder, I thought.

I come all this way from one at work this morning just to go down another.

I left the Bird Taxi stuck in the tree and followed the driver's directions. He said take a right turn at the next side street. Dark warehouses shut for the night lined the sidewalk with fences of slat wood and chain link. More of those tall winter trees stood along the curbside.

I wondered if they heard the news about their comrade who caught the gondola. It was probably big news by now, telegraphed by roots from tree to tree.

Wasn't Pinocchio made from a tree that could talk? I carried his book in my hand and I still haven't opened it. Even with all those miles sitting in the bus, I stared out the window instead of reading. I also took a nap for a while.

Ahead of me, some red traffic lights glowed

and velocipedes stopped in the street.

People with places to go were finding the sidewalk, smudged by a purple neon sign above.

Music was drifting my way. I was headed in the right direction.

I honestly can't remember the last time I went out to a club. When I was younger, I would go see music—now of course I just listen to records. I wasn't sure what to expect at The Broken Gate. I've never seen Cornelius Barter play on stage. We've talked about songs we like, and a couple times he's visited the radio station, but all I knew about what I was walking into was that Pinocchio was in danger.

XIX.
The Broken Gate

Beneath that purple neon there really was a broken gate. It was pinned open against the fence like a wounded butterfly. I wasn't the only one to stand in line, but it suddenly occurred to me: how was I going to get in? I shuffled forward with the line towards the brick saloon, but I was searching the walls for open windows, a fire escape, or some hatch on the roof.

Before I knew it, I was at a ticket window cut in ivy. "Next!"

"Hello," I said. I could already tell she would be a hard sell. She probably heard my story ten times a night. "I just need to get inside to get my friend. He's with Cornelius Barter, but I need to bring him home."

"If you want to get in to the show, you need a ticket."

"I know, but I—look, I don't have the money."

"Then you can't get a ticket," she said. "Next!"

"No! Wait!" I offered the only other thing I had. "Here. This book is worth more than the price of a ticket."

I'm sorry Blue Fairy, I said to myself, as she took the book and gave it a look. "That's a hundred years old," I said. "Look at those illustrations. They don't make books like this anymore."

She sighed, "Alright. You're lucky I like it." She pushed it to the side of her counter and gave me a ticket. "Enjoy the show."

I didn't recognize the loud music filling The Broken Gate, but that's no surprise—I've been locked away in the KGUS studio with the 20th Century. That's all I listen to.

The big dark room was filled with tables. People were gathering in front of the empty stage and everyone was waiting for Cornelius Barter and his band.

I stood by a post where I could view the whole room. There was no sign of Pinocchio, but if he was with Cornelius Barter, wouldn't they be backstage? How was I supposed to get back there?

I took a few steps down onto the main floor and followed the edge of the crowd, along the wall to a door. It was left propped open by a wooden folding chair. Casually, I leaned around a cloud of smoke and peered in. A hallway, another door, and wouldn't you know! That same woman who got my book caught my eye. She motioned for me to come to her so I pushed around the chair.

She looked a lot more worried now as she met me in the green light of the hall. "Didn't you say your friend was with Cornelius Barter?"

"That's right."

"Is your friend a little guy?" she asked, holding her hand at waist height.

"Yes."

She passed me a note. "You better look at this. I found it in the dressing room."

I read the bold letters at the top of the slip, **Dean's Pawn Shop**. It was a receipt. Below that handwriting spelled, *For Talking Puppet*, with a total of *$24*.

She said, "Looks like he sold your friend."

"What do you mean?" I asked. "He pawned Pinocchio?"

"*That's* who he looked like!" she said. "That's why you had that book!"

"Where's Dean's Pawn Shop?"

She rolled her eyes. "You don't want to go there at night."

Something in the room beside us crashed. We both jumped.

There was a muffled cry in there.

"What?" I started to ask, but she hurried around me into the doorway.

She was back in a second. She looked like she had seen an elephant. "You better go in there," she muttered and added, "I just hope we still have a show," and was gone.

The recorded music from the dancehall poured and echoed around me in the hall. I was only a few steps from the dressing room.

The Blue Fairy needed me to be brave, so what else could I do? I took a deep breath and walked in.

Once I saw Pinocchio, the suspense was over and I wasn't even that surprised. Knowing him, it wasn't something you wouldn't expect. He sat on the floor under the open window with his back to the wall, crying and pulling on his long donkey ears.

"Pinocchio!"

"Ohhh…" his voice hitched when he saw me. He rubbed his bright red sleeve across his eyes. He did look pathetic.

"What happened?"

"The same thing that *always* happens to me," he moaned.

I felt sorry for him. I know it seems like I reached the end of my rope with him, but what could I do? I leaned and gave him a hand and pulled him to his feet. He felt like he needed strings to hold him standing, to start him walking again.

I said, "Where's Cornelius Barter?"

"He's gone. He sold me and got what he wanted and now he's off on a cloud."

"What about the concert?"

"Who knows…He doesn't care."

"Well, let's get out of here."

As we took a step towards the door, his wooden shoe fell off and Pinocchio stamped a hoof on the floor. He wobbled and gave a hoarse cry. I caught his arm.

"Oh no," I groaned. "You're not turning into a donkey again, are you?"

"I'm afraid I am." He tugged his ears. "I never should have come here! I should have known better." He stepped out of his other shoe and balanced on two hooves. He was changing fast.

"What happened to you, Pinocchio?"

"I fell in with bad company," he sobbed. "All I wanted was music and adventure and he took me to the pawn shop and sold me and I had to break out of there and Ohhhh!" he cried and brayed, "I don't have long now!"

"What can I do?"

"The ocean. You have to take me to the sea." Pinocchio fell forward as his arms straightened, locked, and became legs. "The water…" he said. Those were his last words. "The wa-wa-wahh-HAWW!"

Right before my eyes he had transformed completely into a small gray donkey.

XXX.
Pinocchio Becomes A Donkey And We Say Goodbye To Cornelius Barter

We didn't wait around. Pinocchio trotted along beside me as we hurried down the hall and out the emergency exit into the alley. Pinocchio was like an obedient dog. It was hard to believe it was him under that animal skin.

I wasn't sure where we were going. I just wanted to get away from the club. It sounded like a riot in there. With no Cornelius Barter in sight, the crowd would be wanting their money back. I heard a bottle break. We followed the alley as it took us along a tall brick warehouse wall. I didn't know the town, but I remembered the way the Bird Taxi took me and I knew if we hooked around the block we could be headed back towards the bus station.

The wild din faded behind as we walked into the sounds of a desolate area of town. Pinocchio's hooves clopped on the broken cement. Crickets trilled in a yard packed with stacks of lumber and sleeping equipment. I thought of the cricket that Pinocchio used to know. I wondered if he was in there with them, calling out to us.

Actually, I liked this part of town. It reminded me of back home. It felt forgotten by the rush on the main street and I kept walking us deeper. We weren't in any hurry. When we got to the bus station we would just take the next bus home. They might not even be running this late at night. I wondered if there was a little house like mine along this alley. Maybe a person like me would invite us in.

At the next corner, we turned to make our way back to the station. The street sparkled with a dusting of broken glass, chips small as stars, and Pinocchio made a pleasant clatter as he walked. Behind it though, I heard a mournful low moan coming from the direction we were headed.

Pinocchio heard it too—of course he did! His ears were five times bigger than mine—and he skittered ahead of me.

"Pinocchio!" I jogged after him. The sound, like a swami calling a cobra from a basket, could turn the next moment into the ring of a beautiful metal flower. Ahead of me, lit by moonlight, Pinocchio hopped on his hind legs beside a high stone wall.

I already knew who sat at the top, almost hovering on the song his trumpet made. When Cornelius Barter played in the alley back home, the world would seem to stop and turn into a swirl.

Pinocchio skipped and danced on the street at the foot of the wall while the strange Humpty Dumpty sight of Cornelius Barter ran through his song oblivious to us.

"Come on, Pinocchio!" I said. I set my hand on top of his head. I knew the song in the air above. It was an old ballad, a love song to love that vanished. "Pinocchio!"

It was like dragging him from the Pied Piper. His four legs were frozen as the limbs of a chair. Pinocchio kept looking over his shoulder until his view was blocked by an unworkable parked car. We stopped in that relic's shadow, the music turned down like a radio, and I could feel that poor cursed wooden donkey returning to life. He shook his head, his floppy ears full of that honeyed sound.

"Are you okay?" I asked. "We only have to go to the end of this street and turn the corner." Pinocchio forced a step forward with me. "That's right. Just don't look back." I made sure. I kept my hand on him and guided him. I know he wanted to go running back to Cornelius. I could feel him fighting the urge, as step by step we got further. I must be immune to the pull of that siren song—living in the alley I've heard him often. Maybe I'm already under the spell.

When we reached the corner, just before we turned onto the next blackened street, I did look back. Cornelius Barter was still playing, slumped, ten feet in the air. I don't know how he floated up there. I don't even know if he was aware.

XXXI.
A Bus Out Of Town Can't Be Found

The rest of the way to the bus station was like taking a dog for a walk. Pinocchio had to stop at the tree where the Bird Taxi tangled up. He sniffed at the spot where I dropped to the ground. There was no sign of my driver or his gondola, but there were snapped branches and a scratch up there on the trunk.

Fortunately there were still lights on in the station. We went inside and stared at the big reader board on the wall. I've seen the kind in old movies that click with city names and times of arrival and departure. This was just a simple blackboard with a few destinations written in chalk. I saw some other places I vaguely know and our city was listed too. Reading that word, I pictured my alley, my little house, and my bed. I told Pinocchio, "We made it here in time for the last bus," and we hurried to the ticket window.

I didn't have my book anymore, but I had our return ticket and some change, enough to buy some chocolate from the vending machine. Do donkeys eat chocolate?

"Where to?" The teller looked like he had never seen the light of day. At dawn he probably slept in a crypt or a rusted wheel well.

I showed him my return ticket. "We're going home."

"Not without another ticket," he croaked. "But we don't let dogs on our bus."

"This isn't a dog. He's a donkey. I mean he's a puppet who turned into a donkey. You've heard of Pinocchio, haven't you?"

My explanation didn't help.

"No animals," he said and I could tell it was final.

So how were we supposed to get home? I put the ticket on the counter and pushed it towards him. "I'd like to get a refund then."

He said, "Read the fine print on your ticket." He turned from me as if he heard a pot of tea boiling in the other room.

When I looked at my ticket, I saw he was right. In letters that tracked across the paper like the footprints left by ants, I read: *No Refunds or Exchanges. Other Restrictions Apply, Including No Animals.*

"Oh brother…" I caught myself from crumpling it. Maybe if the donkey could turn back into Pinocchio we'd be alright. Pinocchio did it before. What did he say? Something about bringing him to the ocean? We were a long way from there. Besides, once we got back to the sea, we'd be home.

"I don't know, Pinocchio," I sighed. "Looks like we're walking."

XXXII.
How To Lose 47¢ In An Alley

I opened the door for Pinocchio and he left the bus station, head hung dejectedly. We didn't get much further than ten paces when a pair of shady looking characters caught up with me.

One of them was tall, thin, all sharp crooked points and he wore a long gray overcoat that looked like it had been hung up high on a wall with him in it. The other guy was short, squat and wore a wide brimmed fedora. His face split in a yellowy grin. "You looking for something?" he said. "Do you need a ticket somewhere?"

In hindsight, it's easy to say we should have kept walking, maybe we could have lost them, but I was so outraged at the prospect of walking all the way out of this town, down a mountainside. I waved the narrow strip of paper and told him, "I have a ticket! But my ticket's no good. They won't let us get on the bus."

He shook his head sympathetically. His tall partner did too, a moment later, in time with each other, like a couple of carved figurines on a cuckoo clock. "That's too bad," the short one said. "But your luck's about to change." The tall mute one suddenly smiled and began to nod. "We can help you get on that bus."

"Really?"

"Sure. Your ticket just needs the right authority stamp on it. With the right stamp, they'd take you to the Moon if you wanted." He held out his hand. "Let me see your ticket."

I let him have a look and he said, "That's the problem alright. But don't you worry. We'll get you that stamp. Follow us."

"Follow us," his partner finally spoke.

"Okay. Come on, Pinocchio." At the time it didn't even seem to me it might not be the best idea, following those two down the dark alley. I just wanted to get home.

"Right over here," said the guy with my ticket.

"This is the place," said the tall one.

They stood beside a metal door set in the scarred bricks under a fire escape stairway. It looked like it hadn't been opened since the Civil War.

"A friend of mine works in there. He's got stamps for every occasion." Prepared to knock on the rusted door, he paused and turned that yellow grin on me again. "Oh, there's just one thing. A favor like this doesn't come cheap. How much money you got?"

I dug in my pocket and showed him all I had was change. It looked like about forty seven cents.

They both laughed.

"I know," I said. "It's been a long day." I handed them the coins. "We really need that stamp."

Still chuckling, the guy with our ticket kneeled and placed it before the door. He arranged the change on top of it to hold it down. The tall guy watched and wheezed like a smokestack. I guess it was laughter. I don't know how funny it is to see all you have in the world laid out before you in a dark alley behind a bus station. Pinocchio leaned against me.

"Okay…" He straightened up and brushed his sleeves. He gazed down at our offering. "Charlie will take care of that."

"Charlie will take care of that," the tall one said with another wheeze.

"Yeah." He rapped three times softly on the door.

Charlie must have tremendous hearing, I thought.

"We'll leave now," the short one said. "Charlie likes his privacy. Let's take a little stroll. When we get back a stamped ticket will be waiting here."

"Really?" I said.

"Sure."

"Sure," echoed the tall one.

We left my ticket and all the money I had. The alley took us back to the street where we started.

"Now we just wait a little bit," I was told. "Watch the pretty cars go by."

We did.

It was a busy street. Lights, traffic, windows.

"Hey Stretch," the shorter fellow finally said. "Why don't you go check on that ticket?"

"I'll see if Charlie is done," he sniffed.

Pinocchio was lying down tired by my feet, but I wanted to follow.

"Don't worry," Stretch's partner said, "He'll be right back with your stamped ticket." He flashed that grin again. I knew it was phony, believe me I knew. We watched the street and waited for Stretch.

XXXIII.
Getting Up In The Morning After Sleeping Under A Bridge

He came back. It's not like he scooped my money and ticket, ran around the block and sold it to some other stranded traveler. Although I guess that's a possibility…When Stretch came back and held his hands out empty, "It's gone," is what he told us.

So that left me and Pinocchio with nothing. I was worn out. The poor donkey at my feet had fallen asleep on the cement. I knew we had to find somewhere we could wait out the night.

Which is how we ended up on a piece of cardboard under a bridge. And we were lucky to have that!

Curled up like a dog, Pinocchio slept beside me.

Not me though, I couldn't sleep. I lay on my back and listened to the rattle and whoosh of traffic above. They were all going home to beds, walls, and warmth that was better than a donkey. They rushed overhead and I tried to believe it was a mountain stream.

That was the only way I could finally close my eyes.

It isn't true to say I woke up.

I was so cold and sore and annoyed that I finally sat up and glared at the dull silver light of the new day. I rubbed my stinging eyes. The black night had gone and I could see where we were.

It was pretty grim. Concrete sloped down from our cardboard bed to a trickling stream. I staggered towards it in the shadow of the bridge's rattling roof. Plants grew beside the water, alongside the trash that wandered there. I picked up an empty peach can. I could fill it with water for Pinocchio.

I stopped beside the water. It was about twenty feet to the other bank of cement. I couldn't tell if it got deep, it was such a dark slow current.

I knelt and patted some water on my face. It felt good and cold.

Not far from me, a mound of blackberry scratched and shook aside where a sort of tunnel funneled out.

First a black dog appeared and then an old lanky man with a red beard turning white.

The dog saw me right away, but it ran towards me in a friendly way.

His owner growled at it, "Pally!" as he straightened up from the ground. I guessed they both lived in there. They carved the blackberry and lived in the middle of it like Br'er Rabbit.

"Pally!"

I was already petting the dog. He wasn't much more than a puppy, wiry, and bouncy as a balloon. "It's okay," I said. The dog jumped around me like a seal. "He's friendly."

"He's friendly and still a fool. Hold still, Pally!" I watched as the man from the brambles slipped a slim rope around his dog. The motion of his hands turning it into a loop was quick and nautical.

"I slept up there last night," I told him, pointing back at the shadow.

He didn't say anything, but he noticed the peach can I held. "You want some tea in that?"

"Oh, sure. Thanks, that sounds good."

"Here," he told me, "You hold Pally for a minute."

I took the rope and he vanished into the blackberries again.

Pally watched the bushes.

"It's okay," I said. "He'll be right back." I hoped he

would. I didn't want to end up wandering about town
with a dog and a donkey. Wasn't there an old story like
that? I remembered. It was the Bremen Musicians. I
was trying to recall how it went when the vines started
shaking again.

Pally gave him a happy bark.

He carried the peach can with his shirt sleeve
pulled and tucked around the hot metal. It sloshed a
bit as he stood back up and he growled at his hand.

I pulled my arm into my sleeve the way he did so I
could take the tea.

"It's hot," he said.

"Thanks."

A teabag steeped in the can. A string tied to it hung
over the edge and fluttered. The little kite of a paper
tag stapled on the end of string read *Good Day.* Drink-
ing tea from a can was a new one for me.

"Do you have a dog?" he asked.

I couldn't speak, my tongue was burned. I turned
my attention from the tin can tea. It was hard to look
him in the eyes—they seemed to burn out of him…
Especially now, as he stared up the cement hill.

"That's the *weirdest* dog I ever saw!" he said. Pally
yapped and strained his rope leash.

By now I saw what they were staring at. Pinocchio,
as if his feet were on roller skates, slowly and carefully
approached us down the slant.

XXXIV.
Pally & Redwood's Plan

Once Redwood and Pally got over their surprise, they seemed pleased to meet my donkey traveling companion. They enjoyed the way Pinocchio danced about and walked on his hind legs like a trained poodle. Even as an animal, he had the talent to win people over and I have to admit I was starting to feel the effects too. I told the whole story, from the day I dug him out of the earth. It sounded crazy, but Redwood nodded and accepted it—he already abandoned reality a long time ago. He even had an idea how we could get back home.

I finished my tea, Pinocchio ate some dandelions, and we said our goodbyes to Redwood and Pally.

"I know you can't talk right now," I told Pinocchio as we walked along, "But I sure hope we don't have to spend another night like that."

Pinocchio gave his best attempt at an answer, a raspy bray that I took as a yes.

It was a pleasant morning, the sun was out, and it felt good to have a plan. Redwood's directions were spot on. It didn't take long before we saw the spires of big trees rising over the roofs of houses.

We crossed one more street and a beautiful big park started a block away.

Pinocchio had seen me press the crosswalk button before and this time he insisted he try, hopping on his back legs to tap the post with his hoof. He was really getting agile in his new form. People leaned out of their cars to stare. Wheels and bicycles slowed. I had to admit Redwood's idea to get us home just might work.

XXXV.
Pinocchio Shows Off At The Circus

I haven't been to a circus since I was a kid and this one wasn't like the one I remember. Maybe it's just the passing of time and what I've seen since then—it takes more than a few tents, clowns and animals to excite me anymore. That's probably a little sour to admit, I'm sorry. I just wanted to be home.

But Pinocchio was in his element. His excited antics were already drawing the attention of some of the circus workers. One by one, they left what they were doing.

I waved as we approached. It wasn't me they were watching though—it was the donkey, tossing himself about like a toy. "Take it easy, Pinocchio," I hissed. I didn't want him to land on his head, even though the ground around us was grassy and covered with dandelions and tiny white and pink daisies. It looked comfortable actually—a lot better than sleeping on concrete under a bridge. I could go to sleep on it right now.

"That's quite a donkey," said someone close to me.

Pinocchio broke from me and danced around three men in overalls. He purred up against a woman who looked like an acrobat, then off he went again, spinning and cavorting.

"Did you train him?"

I nodded and lied, "Yes. He obeys my commands." And I took a chance. "Pinocchio! Freeze!"

He did. We were all surprised. He was stuck to the lawn like a park statue.

I let him stand that way a moment more then

ordered, "Pinocchio! Dance!"

Immediately, he was a flurry.

"That's very impressive. Your donkey is a natural performer." While everyone else gathered about Pinocchio laughing and clapping, this wiry looking circus old-timer introduced himself to me. "My name is Burke. I run the animals here."

I don't know how I worked my nerve up to this situation—I went from being a shy, clay digging alley dreamer to a circus huckster. I told him, "Would it be possible to loan out Pinocchio's services for your next show? All I'm asking is enough money for a train ticket, or to rent a Wheel to get us back home."

He thought about it. He rubbed his chin and watched Pinocchio.

XXXVI.
The Old Detective & The Mermaid

Everywhere Pinocchio went he made friends. It didn't even matter what form he was in. And what used to drive me up the wall about him was starting to grow on me too. He wasn't so bad. People liked him, didn't they? He made them laugh as he balanced on the tent ropes. When we sat for lunch Pinocchio used the table as a stage. He never tired from being on. A clown gave him a red cone hat just like the one he used to wear as a puppet.

It wore me out watching him though.

After lunch I went looking for somewhere to nap.

With a bit of hunting around behind a tent, next to the canvas billow I discovered a pillow of hay. I collapsed upon it and sleep came at me like an ocean wave.

I didn't know where I lay, or if I dreamed at all. Then it was like reincarnation the way I was suddenly thrust into the world again. I felt like an old detective, blackjacked and waking in the gutter. I would have thought I was in hell but the lady hovering over me with a pitchfork was no devil.

"Who are you?" she said.

Oh God, I was so tired.

"You're on the elephant's hay." She waved the pitchfork.

"I'm sorry." I slowly got to my feet.

"Do you work here?"

"No. I'm here with Pinocchio the donkey." I brushed off some hay.

"They love that donkey."

"Well, I hope so. We need to get home."

"You better watch out though. They might want him to stay."

I almost laughed, thinking that was a joke, the sort of ominous line you'd hear in a black and white movie. I imagined her in those clothes from the 1940s—a dress and soft fedora hat, with her earrings sparkling and sending out rays over the audience.

"I'm serious," she said. "This circus does what it can to survive. That donkey's going to be a star. They already have me making posters of him."

"You're kidding."

She plunged the pitchfork into the stack of hay. "Follow me, I'll show you."

She led me along the tent, past the Mermaid tank. It was parked out of sight, the aquarium hidden by painted boards. I wished I could stop and take a look. I've never seen a mermaid.

Around the side of the next tent we stopped next to her car. She opened the door and I could see the stacks of signs on the front seat. She picked them up and fanned them a little so I could see each one was different, hand-painted by her. There was a quick bright picture of a donkey in the middle surrounded by words—*The Saturn Circus Presents Pinocchio: The World Famous Donkey.* I must have looked hypnotized.

She said, "I have to go around town and put these up. You want to join me?"

XXXVII.
We Spend Too Much Time Talking About Pinocchio

I wish I had a camera. For the next couple hours we had our own adventure and each time I caught her eyes and smile, I wished I had a picture to last all my life. All those songs I play at night were coming true.

I actually didn't feel alone in the world.

I told her about the Bird Taxi and showed her the tree and we put a poster on it for everyone to see.

We stopped at a café she knew and she ordered a pot of tea for us. I still didn't have a cent to my name and she laughed when I told her the story why. She couldn't believe how I was hoodwinked.

I changed the subject. I wanted to know more about her. I said I loved her painting, "You should be making art all the time. Do you like working for the circus?"

"I can't make a living just doing paintings. I also have chores to do. The circus is my job. But I try to make time my art whenever I can."

And then I told her my theory. "People arrive on Earth with their talents. If it's art and they aren't able to share it, the world suffers. Without art the world is a sorry place."

The tea arrived and she poured us each a cup. "What about you?" she asked. "What are you doing hanging around with a donkey?"

"Oh, I don't do that for a living. I'm just trying to get us home so he can turn back into a puppet."

"So he really is Pinocchio?"

"He really is."

"Why is he a puppet again? Wasn't he supposed to turn into a boy?"

"Don't ask me. I still don't know the whole story." I took a sip of tea. It was mint and something.

We talked more. I wanted to hear all about her. I could have listened all day. I need more than a camera for this feeling, or a phonograph—no—I didn't need anything but her. I hoped she wasn't the Blue Fairy. Wouldn't that be just my luck, to find out she isn't even real?

Then she sighed and pushed at her empty cup. "We better go. I have to get back to my water."

"What water?"

"The water in my aquarium."

"Oh," I said. I figured it was just another chore, like the hay for the elephant. Little did I know…

XXXVIII.
Something Is Always Happening

We rushed along a street that was pink with blossoming cherry trees. Somehow I hadn't noticed spring arrive and now it was everywhere, all around us. Flowers were poking through cracks in sidewalks, birds were singing again. We were doing our part too, sitting close together, driving circles in town. It was too bad we couldn't stay under those branches though.

With the park arriving in sight I knew we were about to parachute back into a hurried circus getting ready for the show and I might not see her like this again. I didn't want our time to end. I wished the circus would whirl away and leave us alone on a grassy field. But I felt lucky just the same. Our day would be remembered. In my memory it had been pressed and turned into one of those ballad records I love to play.

The car ended up where we started, beside the tent. The sun made long shadows on the canvas, with ropes, poles, and a tree silhouette that branched like wallpaper.

I said, "Bye," and, "I hope I see you again."

She waved and laughed, "You will," and, "I have to go."

Things were happening—things were always happening—but this time it felt like a door opened to somewhere I had never been.

XXXIX.
One of the Oldest Jokes In Clown History

It wasn't easy to think of Pinocchio again but when she was gone and I was alone, I remembered him and went looking.

Before I left for the day I could have followed the laughter to find that donkey. Now it was a different story. We were only an hour from show time, everyone had somewhere to be and something to do. Except for me.

I stopped a clown and asked, "Have you seen Pinocchio the donkey?"

I guess I should have picked a different clown. He soaked me with a plastic flower stuck in the lapel of his checkered jacket. That's got to be one of the oldest jokes in clown history, but he waddled away pleased as punch.

Fine.

I walked by the tent where we had our lunch. An elephant was in there getting painted with stars. A magician wearing a top hat was pushing legs into a box. No donkeys though…Maybe I had been a bad guardian, leaving him here so I could run around the day with a beautiful girl, but wasn't he able to care for himself?

Of course he wasn't.

I kept looking for him. That book of his was one long example of how he couldn't care for himself. Wasn't that the whole point of Pinocchio? And I had been warned too—the circus wanted him to stay.

When I turned another canvas corner, I practically

ran right into Burke. He was bent into the sawdust like a rusted nail.

"I'm looking for Pinocchio." I didn't want to sound anxious, but here I was going into another night away from home on what should have been a simple rescue mission. I'm sure Bruno was fuming.

Burke told me, "He's with the dancing horses. We ran him through the act and he fits like a glove."

"Can I go see him?"

"This isn't a good time. They're preparing for the show. I'll tell you what though, here's a couple of tickets. Bring a friend, see the act for free." He offered them to me and nodded brusquely. "I have to get going. Still got things to do."

"Okay. See you later."

What was I supposed to do with an extra ticket? I don't know anyone else in this town.

XL.
Wandering Around

I just wandered around. I saw the tent where Pinocchio would be performing, but I had time before the flap would open for the show. I watched animals in carriages rolled into the big tent. The mermaid's boarded up aquarium appeared, pulled by an elephant. They went slowly to keep the water from sloshing down the sides. There was a long aisle where booths were set up on either side. I heard the first popping cracks from the shooting gallery, testing the guns. Bells and music, balloons and the aromas of food filled the air. When the gates opened, all of a sudden there were people flooding in everywhere. This whole town has been waiting for the circus to come.

XLI.
47¢, Pinocchio Tickets, The Criminal Element

A long time ago, when I first moved to the alley, I used to sit at the abandoned department store lunch counter, leaning on the formica turned gray with age, all the silver trim dull. I swiveled my chair and imagined what it must have been like. The ghosts were so close I could feel their America brushing against me. If they could get electricity back in the lights, in the radio, in the stoves and fans turning in the kitchen, I'm sure those people would pop right back to life. The place was haunted without them, but I also liked it— the quiet, gloomy stillness was peaceful and thoughtful.

It was a startling change from where I now found myself, standing outside the circus tent with a crowd of people jostling around me.

From a wooden stage next to the entrance flap, I could hear Burke's sales pitch, "See twenty dancing horses, featuring the little wonder of the world, Pinocchio! Thrills, comedy, amazement! Tickets now on sale!"

That's when I saw two familiar faces from the bus station. They were eyeing the crowd for suckers, the same way they did for me last night. When they spotted me, they grinned, like seeing an old friend.

"Are we glad to see you!" the shorter one said. "Stretch, show him what we found."

"We got back the money you lost."

"Forty seven cents!" Stretch's friend said. "We found the guy who stole it. He put up quite a fight."

Stretch passed me the coins.

What a surprise! I was so glad I was wrong about them.

Stretch's friend pointed at the tent. "Are you seeing this show? I sure wish we could…But now we gave you that money, we can't pay for tickets…"

"That's okay." I dropped the change back in Stretch's hand. "I don't need the money. Pinocchio is getting paid to perform. You keep it."

"Thanks," Stretch told me.

His short friend sighed, "It still isn't enough for two tickets though."

"Oh," I remembered, "I have two tickets. You can have these. I don't need them, I know the trainer. He'll let me in."

They were very pleased.

Stretch laughed. "I can't wait to see Pinocchio. I wish I had a pet like that."

I didn't know the shorter guy's name yet, but he said, "Hey, maybe after the show we can take a look at Pinocchio up close?" He shook his head in wonder. "Imagine having a donkey like that!"

"Yeah," Stretch said. "Imagine that."

XLII.
Where A Jar Full of Coins Would Have Really Helped

That left me in a predicament. Without a ticket, I needed Burke to get in the tent, but he went inside to start the show, leaving someone else to guard the entrance. It was someone who swung a mallet and smoked cigarettes for a living. It was someone who didn't believe that I knew Burke and that the donkey in the act was mine. When there was a fanfare and applause, the show began without me.

Standing not six feet from the tied flaps, I could imagine the string of ponies dancing before the crowd, with little Pinocchio leading the way. More applause erupted. It occurred to me that Stretch and his partner got my money again too, with my tickets. I don't think of myself as gullible, but in this town I had lost everything and then some. And didn't it sound like they were also after Pinocchio? On top of everything else, I couldn't lose Pinocchio. I would have to find another way into the tent.

Like some bit of flotsam in the stream, I flowed with the crowd alongside the tent. Booths were crowded beside it. With a little money I could have leaned on the counter and bought food or tried my luck at some random winning game.

I must have had that destitute look though for none of the barkers tried to catch my eye and as I went by I tried not to look.

If you must know, I watched the ground. Sometimes people drop coins. Back home I found enough in the alley to fill a jar. Too bad I didn't have them here.

At the end of the aisle and the booth at the corner of the tent, I stopped. I waited to cut around the back where I hoped the acts would be leaving when they were done.

All I had to do was slip past the last big carriage parked there.

XLIII.
The Mermaid's House

The blue painted boards glistened with spilled water and I took a moment to read the lettering. *Captured Live From the Ocean's Depth.* I don't know why, but I placed my hand flat against the mermaid's tank. I don't know if I expected an electric current or instant enlightenment from some unseen mystery. Nothing like that happened.

I followed the painting of a fish tail around the carriage to the other side where the tail turned into a woman. Her face was familiar—I had spent the day with her.

I smiled. I liked that she painted herself as a mermaid.

She held a shell in one hand and her other hand pointed at a round window.

I couldn't resist. Nobody was around to stop my curiosity.

It was just a round piece of glass framed in brass over a dark circle on the carriage wall, but it was a great effect. If I was ten, I would have spent a long time staring, watching for a fish, or the waving arm of an octopus. I was the sort of kid who would believe anything. In spite of the years, that hasn't changed much. Faith in the imaginary is what got me here.

So you wouldn't expect that little so-called window to give me such a jump. Something floated suddenly into view. The green face of my friend looked back at me. Her long hair flowed around her like kelp leaves.

"Is that you?" I said. Was this why she had to hurry back to the water? Would her legs only last so long before she needed to plunge into the aquarium and return to the sea? She smiled and a bubble left her mouth. She looked so cheery, like someone looking out of her home. Was it like an underwater house in there, with furniture? Who was she anyway? I had only known her a couple of hours.

She pointed up towards the surface. There were shells in a bracelet around her wrist. Then she swam past the window and her long green body went by smoothly, tapering into a scaled tail and fins. She really dressed the part!

I heard a splash above me and water seeped down across the painted siding. "Hey!" she called me.

I left the porthole. I stepped back and shielded my eyes against the arc lighting of the circus night sky. On this backside of the tank there was a tall leaning ladder. She must have climbed that to get in.

"Hi!" She peered over the edge. She was fifteen feet above me.

I don't know if I would have climbed that ladder to see her. I'm sure I would have, but I didn't get the chance.

XLIV.
I Am Responsible For A Donkey

Loud applause inside the tent with a brassy fanfare interrupted us and I turned to see horses emerge from the canvas. They gathered behind the tent on a lawn surrounded by parked trailers.

"I have to go," I said. I could see Pinocchio darting among the tired performers and I didn't want to lose track of him. It didn't look like he was in danger, but who really knew? I hurried over the grass, dodging the wooden stakes. Funny how it felt to see him after hours apart, like one of those parents coming from a long day at work to get their kid at school.

"Pinocchio!" I kneeled down and held my arms out.

The donkey trotted between two horses and raced towards me, almost knocking me over as he planted two hooves on my leg. I caught myself and gave him a hug.

I know. What a sight…

"It's good to see you," I almost cried.

He gave me a look that must have meant the same. But then he was distracted by the appearance of Burke who stood next to us holding out a handful of corn.

"Wasn't he something?" Burke laughed. "Seems like he's been doing this all his life."

Pinocchio ate greedily and allowed Burke to take the bright costume saddle off his back.

"The crowd really loves this little donkey," Burke continued. "Listen…" he stopped scratching Pinocchio, "How much would you want for him?"

"I can't sell him. He's not mine. We just wanted to

do one show."

Burke's eyes narrowed as he said, "Name your price."

"I'm sorry. He's not for sale." I took a step in front of Pinocchio. He was happy as can be. Now he was uprooting dandelions. It wasn't easy for me to say, "If you can pay us for his work, we'll be on our way."

I was surprised though when Burke laughed and put his hand on my shoulder. "Of course. You two stop by my trailer. If you ever change your mind, you know where we are. Give me a half hour. I just need to get these horses put away."

"Okay," I said, adding, "thanks." I don't know what I was so worried about. "Well, Pinocchio," I sighed, "Looks like we can go back home."

He stopped eating flowers and stared at me. Did he want to stay?

I said, "Sorry you can't always do what you want to."

I'm sure he was telling me how much he loved the circus.

"You have to be in that car commercial, remember?"

He remembered. He cast his eyes at the cropped grass and stamped his hoof. I could see he wasn't happy about it. I wasn't either. It's not easy having responsibilities. In his book, Pinocchio always had the hardest time with that. Oh well…We still had a long way to go. I looked up and saw the moon. Not that far at least…

XLV.
Stretch & Cavendish Chase Us Up A Ladder

"Hey!" A yell shot our way. "There you are!"

That voice startled us. Pinocchio pressed close to my leg as Stretch approached.

"We've been looking for you," he said. He glanced over his shoulder then back at Pinocchio. The poor donkey hid behind me. Being an animal, he must have been able to pick up on more than me—there was an unseen tension deflected by the neon lights and calliope.

I said, "What do you want?"

"We want that donkey." Out of the blue, he gave me a shove that sent me falling over and he reached down for Pinocchio.

I rolled and was getting to my feet as Pinocchio gave Stretch a powerful kick.

Now Stretch was on the ground, crying out, "Cavendish!" holding his wrist, tangled in a rope by the tent.

I grabbed Pinocchio and ran.

I held him in my arms like a baby, careful not to trip or skid on the uneven ground.

Behind us I heard Stretch scream, "Cavendish!" again. I supposed that was the name of his short accomplice, but I didn't want to find out. You would have thought I knew just what I was doing as I made a beeline for the mermaid's tank and climbed that ladder. I held Pinocchio under my arm, clutched like a suitcase. The ladder bounced under my weight as I climbed.

"Louise!" I called. I didn't know if she was still in there. I had no idea what manner of illusion the tank contained. Once I reached the top and could look over the edge, I was surprised to find it filled with deep looking water, black as outer space. "Louise!"

Stretch was still bellowing for Cavendish, though the sound was fading.

Pinocchio squirmed so I rested him on the ledge. He was heavier than you would think. He wasn't made of wood anymore. "Louise! Are you there?"

The black surface swirled. Close enough to touch, she appeared, her long hair and shoulders all slick and shiny with moonlight. I don't know what she was up to, floating so easily in that box of ocean.

"Louise. We need your help." That's all I managed to say.

Pinocchio knew what to do. He gave a little kick and hopped out of my hold. His hooves scraped and clattered on the wooden rim as he turned into a splash and sunk.

Louise gave a surprised look then she snapped over into a steep dive. Her tail flashed, cut the water and she was gone too.

XLVI.
Pinocchio Becomes A Marionette Once More. Louise Disappears

There was nothing to see, only the whorl they left behind disturbed the surface. As that flattened into the gentlest creases, I called her name again, "Louise?"

I don't know how long a donkey can hold its breath—not that he was a real donkey—underneath he was a puppet, but hidden in that somewhere was a living boy. What was happening?

I thought of returning to the ground to look through that porthole again, but how would that help? I could only stand there leaning over the water, hoping the mermaid would return him.

Around me I could hear the circus sounds. Twenty feet in the air, that atmosphere drifted about me like pollen. What was missing was that repeating yell for Cavendish. I supposed they were looking for us, probably creeping towards my ladder.

But I didn't care. I didn't turn around. I stared hard at the water.

Louise reappeared silently on the far side of the tank. She moved through the little waves effortlessly and smiled. "Look who's back," she said. She raised that familiar puppet into the air.

He lay in her hands in his bright clothes, crumpled like a flower. His eyes were closed. Then they opened. He grinned and held out his arms to me.

"Pinocchio!" It didn't even cross my mind that I started to cry. I held his small body tightly and he hugged me with all his might.

When the ladder shook, I almost lost my balance.

I held Pinocchio in one hand and grabbed the ledge of the tank. I almost became Humpty Dumpty.

A voice from below asked me, "Where's the donkey, friend?" The ladder shook again. Pinocchio went limp.

I turned and saw Stretch and Cavendish on the hard ground. Stretch had his broken arm wrapped and tied in a hasty sling. They both looked perturbed.

"Where's the donkey?" Stretch repeated.

"We want him," said Cavendish.

"Pinocchio is safe with the other animals," I told them. "Burke, the trainer is watching him."

"That old string bean?" Cavendish laughed. "We'll go pay him a visit, won't we Stretch?" He gave the ladder one last shake before they left. "Don't drop your dolly." They walked away laughing.

Louise swam in place with her chin above the water. "You need to leave this circus," she said. "You need to leave now."

"How?"

"You can borrow my car. Drive to your town. The circus will be there in a couple days. I can pick it up from you then."

"What about Burke? Should I make sure he's okay?"

She shook her wet head. "Burke can take care of them. You need to go. You know where my car is parked. I'll see you in two days." She must have known I would have kept talking. I wasn't ready to leave Louise behind until she slipped beneath the air.

XLVII.
We Say Goodbye To The Circus And Pinocchio Gets Hungry

The only time I ever drive a car is in my dreams. It's always one of those ancient automobiles from the old black and white movies.

Her car wasn't like that. Parts of her car were covered in tin plating and cardboard. Our ticket out of the circus rattled and bumped from side to side every bump we hit.

Pinocchio was in the backseat under a blanket.

I had my collar turned up like Count Dracula.

A narrow lane between ropes took us to the street where we entered traffic. I had a little trouble shifting gears and I have to admit there was some swearing as I tried to speed up. I wasn't worried about offending Pinocchio though—he had heard much worse in his time at the circus.

As I glanced at the rearview mirror, the yellow lit tents, the neon and searchlights, I wondered what happened to Stretch and Cavendish. I had a feeling Burke pounded them into the earth like tent stakes, but I hoped not. I barely knew them. They probably had some sad excuse that had driven them to petty crime. Starting tomorrow, maybe they intended to be respectable and get jobs in a hotel kitchen.

"Is it safe?" Pinocchio asked.

"I guess so."

He popped up and looked out the oval back window.

"Say goodbye to the circus," I hoped. I still didn't see a sign for the road out. I sort of remembered the way the bus went.

I took a quick look in the mirror at Pinocchio. I felt like a taxi cab driver making small talk. "How did you turn back into a puppet?"

"It's the sea water! It happened to me once before when I was a donkey. I—Hey! What's that?" He was pressed against the window, staring at the sidewalk.

"Someone selling pretzels."

"Oooh! Let's stop!"

"Not a chance," I told him. "Besides, we don't have any money, remember?"

Pinocchio sighed loudly. I could see him watching the pretzel stand vanish in the crowds. "Do we have any pretzels at home?"

"No. I can't remember the last time I had a pretzel." It made me hungry though.

"Can we get one next time we have money?"

I said, "Sure. Look! There's a sign for the freeway!" I also got another glimpse of the Bird Taxi. It pulled itself along the letters of a grocery store sign.

"Too bad there's no food in this car," Pinocchio mumbled.

I agreed, though it was weird that a puppet needed to eat. Still, I guess under that wooden skin, he was human somehow. I tried to remember how he turned from marionette to boy. Wasn't the Blue Fairy involved? All I had was a vague intuition how his story went, and I traded away the user's manual to get him out of that jazz club. Still, I had him right here in the car with me—it was going to be a long drive—I could ask him anything I didn't know. "How did you end up in America anyway?"

XLVIII.
The Story of Pinocchio & The Italian Fliers

"*Senti*…When I was in Italy, I was a star. Everyone adored me. I was even invited to the palace in Rome," Pinocchio sighed. "I was different then. I was more of a loudmouth. I was a liar a lot of the time. I'd like to think that 83 years underground let me become a better person. But maybe not, since I'm a puppet again." He sighed once more. I had never seen him so tired. The shadows back there flitting over him gave him the look of an old reel of film.

"Anyway, Il Duce Mussolini liked me. Everyone liked me. Mussolini wanted me to be an ambassador of good will and go to America. So I waved goodbye to my Roma. It was July of 1933, it was a beautiful summer. I can still see it. *Arrivederci Italia!* We left the sea in 25 flying boats. Can you imagine? I was in the lead plane with the Minister of the Air Force, Italo Balbo. The other airplanes strung behind us, shining over Europe, Amsterdam, Ireland, across the North Sea to Iceland. I could stand in the wind beside the pilot and see all that blue ocean going on and on to the horizon. It was glorious!

"Our destination was Chicago, United States of America, The Century of Progress Exposition, but I never made it there. By the time we got to the continent, Balbo had me moved to another plane. I was back in the number thirteen. My new pilot was a fascist and was he ever mean! He would make me walk out on the wing to check the oil in the engines. I had to hang on with all my might out in the wind. It was terrifying! He was always mad at me. He didn't care that I was the beloved Pinocchio, he hated me! And then one night I brought him his coffee and I spilled it. That was the last straw. He grabbed me and threw me off the plane! Can you believe it?"

Pinocchio stopped talking abruptly and I was afraid he was going to start crying. I was sorry for all the ill will I felt towards him in the past. I had been cruel and in my own way as uncaring as that fascist pilot.

He took a deep breath.

We were out on the highway by this time. I followed red taillights and across the black median were the white pearling lights of approaching cars. I wished for some music, but I gave Pinocchio his quiet to recover.

When he was ready, he started his story again. "So I fell. Down and down."

I saw the silhouette of him with his arms outstretched. He really was a ham. But the spotlight suited him. I know it sounds crazy, but Pinocchio had what you would call a magnetic personality. Also, he seemed to be indestructible.

He continued, "I don't remember hitting the ground. I just dreamed for 83 years until you got me out of the clay. Thanks again, by the way."

What could I say?

"It's funny," Pinocchio sighed. For the longest time, I could hear that shovel getting closer. I knew I just had to be patient and wait."

XLIX.
Pinocchio & The Hitchhiker

It was quiet.

Louise's car was doing alright on the highway. It was faster than my Wheel and nice to be sitting out of the weather. When I told Pinocchio I couldn't believe Louise just gave us her car like that, he laughed and said, "Awww, she likes you!" Maybe. I don't know…It was nice to think about.

We were out in a place where the moon was huge and shining on the plowed fields.

It was one of those rare moments on the highway when there were no other cars or trucks around. You were alone with your thoughts and free to let them wander. I was thinking about Louise. I pictured her tomorrow night on this stretch of road, boxed up in her aquarium with the seawater tilting and sloshing. Maybe she had a comfortable chair she could sit in and watch out the porthole at the passing land.

I saw an old billboard in a field and thought of painting it with her name.

Pinocchio spotted something else though—leaning over the back seat, he flung out his wooden stick of an arm and pointed ahead, "Look! That guy on the road wants a ride!"

Our headlights shined on the person, but who could they be out here at night? We had been past the Indian reservation, the tulip fields, and the farmhouses weren't nearby. Only the distant row of mountains were watching us.

"Slow down!" Pinocchio ordered. "I think he's got a bag of bread."

"What?"

"I'm still hungry! If he's not a mirage, you better stop."

I saw him too. He stepped back as we passed, while we pulled off the road, braking onto the shoulder gravel.

He was carrying a shape that did look like a plastic bread bag. He also held something else. I couldn't tell what it was, a package or something. Did he wander the roads at night making sandwiches for whoever stopped? Was he carrying the ingredients all rolled up tight? I hoped this would be a story like that. We wouldn't have long to find out.

"Here he comes!" Pinocchio said.

I reached over and opened the passenger door.

L.
The Road Gets So Steep We Have To Get Out And Push

He looked like he had been waiting to get home all day. Of course, I felt the same way.

He seated himself and placed his belongings on his lap and stared at the windshield. He had stepped off the road, into a car, and now he was ready to go.

So I pressed the pedal and we were on the way.

As we gained speed, we rattled from the shoulder back onto the road. A car passed by on the other side of the median spreading a brief fan of white light.

"You want some bread?" he asked me.

"That sounds good," I said, "We're so hungry. We've been talking about food for miles."

"I meant do you want some money?" he said. "Or you can have bread if you want."

I laughed. "Bread to eat sounds better. If that's okay," I added.

He unwrapped a blanket off what he had been carrying and moved that object onto the dashboard so it looked back at us. It was a carved wooden mask.

The mask looked like a bear staring at me from the windshield.

"That's okay." He untwisted the tie on the bag and passed me a slice.

"Thanks."

He turned and looked at the backseat. "Does your friend want one?"

I could see Pinocchio in the mirror. He stood rigidly in the middle of the seat, staring ahead at the mask.

"Oh," I said, "You can put a piece back there. He got quiet all of a sudden."

"Did you carve him?"

"No. I found him in the ground." I know the situation looked weird, someone driving a puppet around. I took a bite of bread.

He retied his bread bag. He took his time.

The road started to get steep. It almost seemed to be connected to the slow motion twisting of that bag, as if there were unseen pulley wires at work.

"Did you carve that mask?" I asked him.

"No. My cousin did. He is Haida. He gave it to me and I'm taking it home."

I finished my bread. I nodded. "That's what I'm doing too, trying to take Pinocchio back home."

Louise's car gave a groan. It didn't seem to like climbing the road.

I shifted into third gear. The lights on the dash blinked.

I could tell her car wasn't happy. The circus must not go into the mountains much. We were still losing speed on the grade. I was starting to think we might not even make it to the top.

This was the same road that the bus took bringing us to town, but I couldn't remember it being this steep coming down. Now it felt like a rollercoaster. I wanted to say something about it, but all my words had drained behind us. You could open the car trunk and find a whole pile of scrambled questions like, "What's happening to us?" and "Do you think we should stop?"

We were going so slowly, pretty soon we would be going backwards. I didn't know what to do, but fortunately our passenger did.

He opened his door and stepped out. He held to the frame of Louise's car and pushed.

I opened my door too so I could help. I could lean against the car and still keep a hand on the steering wheel.

It was like walking up a slanted ladder.

And I don't know why that bear mask didn't fall off the dashboard! Everything else in the car was clattering around like a snow globe.

I heard, "We're almost there," from the other side of the car. I have no idea how we kept from plummeting backwards off into the steep abyss behind us. Just don't fall, I told myself and somehow we didn't.

LI.
Downhill From The Hilltop Motel

Imagine you're a snail climbing up the leg of a table, shouldering that weight of your shell and then all of a sudden all that steep gravity levels off and you have reached the tabletop.

We steered the car off the highway, onto the edge of the tar and stopped. I killed the engine. I caught my breath listening to the calm of the tall fir trees packed around. Way up above us, a breeze moved branches ever so subtly. This was the closest I'd been to the sky. Bright stars flicked among the clouds.

On the other side of the car, our passenger collected his bread off the seat and his wooden Haida mask. He stood back up and behind his silhouette I could see passage between the trees to a tall neon sign, Hilltop Motel. A faint green light haloed it. "That's enough travel for me today," he said.

I laughed. "Well, I hope it's all downhill from here."

It was.

The rest of the drive was easy, following the headlights, running with the road as if we were just one more scrap of flotsam in a river.

LII.
Pinocchio Answers The Telephone

Pinocchio and I rolled into the alley not too long before dawn. What a drive! I felt like a ghost falling out of the car, but Pinocchio was petrified. Ever since that mask appeared on the dashboard, he had been frozen. He didn't say a word the rest of the way home, which as you might know by now is unheard of.

I parked and reached over the seat and lifted him out. I had to carry him like a stick of firewood.

Thinking he might be asleep, I said, "We're home, Pinocchio." There was no reaction. He looked like any other doll you might see. Wasn't it possible he was just extremely tired? After all we had been through, I could barely unlock the door and stagger inside.

I set Pinocchio on the kitchen table. I put a napkin over him for a blanket. It took the last of my strength to get myself to bed.

Then the telephone woke me.

Sleep had been and gone that quickly.

I listened to the phone ring again and then I heard Pinocchio speak.

"Bonjourno!"

I sat up.

I could see him on the kitchen table holding the phone to his ear.

"We just got back," he said.

As if scalded, he tore the phone from his ear. I could hear the tinny roar of my brother's screams. Pinocchio tried to interrupt, "We…There was…I…" but there was no point in trying to stop a volcano. Bruno would burn until he was done.

I walked into the kitchen, avoiding the telephone, and I poured a pan full of water and set it on the stove.

A breath must have been taken on the other end of the line because Pinocchio had a chance to speak. "We'll be there as soon as we can." I heard a squawk in the receiver. "No," Pinocchio said, "I'm not lying. We'll be there soon."

I stared at the water. I spent years listening to that voice. We would need coffee to face Bruno.

"Okay," Pinocchio said.

I stared at the water and thought of Louise instead. Pinocchio said, *"Ciao!"*

Where was she? What was she doing right now?

"Goodbye," said Pinocchio and he hung up the phone at last.

The first bubble had formed in the pan.

LIII.
Lynden Milan Returns

We had time for a cup of coffee. Pinocchio had a few sips from a china cup but he didn't seem to need it. I remembered his state last night, when he shut down completely. That was curious. I still suspect that was a reaction to the mask, but I didn't ask. Honestly, it was a miracle we survived the night.

I refilled my coffee and soon we left the house.

Pinocchio said everyone was waiting for us at work. He was a little agitated. I felt like I was sleep walking. If I was lucky, I was still dreaming and this wasn't really happening. If only…

I paused after I shut the door and stared. The alley was furred with dew and the day's new light. It looked like a memory.

If only I didn't have to go rushing off. If only I could stand there like a tree and soak it in slowly— this moment, followed by another minute, ten minutes, an hour, the afternoon—isn't that what trees do? They're put in a spot to observe, like a periscope grown from the ground.

Pinocchio, who as usual had hopped ahead of me, caught my attention. He waved his arms and pointed.

Beside Louise's car stood Lynden Milan. It's almost June and there he was again, wanting to shut off the water supply. I should have known better—last night I parked her car next to the water meter. Poor Lynden couldn't make sense of it. So little changed in the alley he didn't know what to do.

I sped to the car, grabbing Pinocchio on the way. "Hello Lynden."

He was speechless, which as I've said before is just as well. Struggling with a sentence he had never used, he looked as if we had come from the moon and before his mind was completely lost, I hurried to put Pinocchio in the backseat and quickly got behind the steering wheel.

I waved to Lynden, though I know in his condition we were as weird as time travelers.

Not surprisingly, his response was to shield his eyes with his hand and wait for us to remove our futuristic, out-of-place intrusion.

I backed Louise's car into the alley. As we left, sure enough, I could see the little figure of Lynden in the mirror, uncovering his eyes. There was a limit to your reliance on the past. Lynden was back where he belonged, where everything was understood.

LIV.
My Last Day At Geppetto Auto Repair

It didn't look like much had changed at work since we left.

The yellow film truck was parked where it was before, along with all the usual vehicles and piles of scrap.

We drove around back of the office and parked by the garage. The door was open, the lights were on, Tock stood at his worktable, already banging away at some broken part.

I turned the engine off and listened to the clang, clang, clang, and I was so tired I closed my eyes. Sleep was only a minute away, until Pinocchio rattled the door handle and chirped, "Come on! *Andiamo!*"

With a sigh, I got out of the car and he scampered right by me, galloping across the gravel towards the shop.

I looked the other way, at the wall of clay. I imagined crawling in there for a long, hundred year nap.

The hammering stopped and I heard Tic Toc's loud hurray. Was he ever glad to see Pinocchio return! I heard little wooden feet dancing about while my brother slapped his metal hands together. I heard the office door swing open as the rest of them in there all came rushing out, crying his name.

No, this was not the time for sleep.

I had to go be a part of this thing happening.

I turned around and there they were, like the actors on stage in a play. Bruno held Pinocchio up in his arms and laughed. I walked towards them, barely keeping my feet from dragging.

I was in no hurry to go back to the work of auto repair, but it seemed that neither were they. My brother Bruno barked out orders and before I reached the garage, he led the entourage back inside the office.

Everyone was gone except for Arlis. That was a surprise to me—I thought she would have been running in Bruno's wake, taking notes and phone calls.

"Welcome back," she said. She held out a paper cup of coffee for me.

"Oh, thanks."

She said, "I hear you didn't get much sleep."

"This is the only thing keeping me awake." I took a sip. Arlis's coffee had a certain notoriety—you could pour it on a cemetery and bring the skeletons to life. I gasped. "That hits the spot!"

"We better get going. I don't want to miss that commercial."

I followed her past the table piled with shining fake metal. That's all I had waiting for me while I was gone. I switched the hot cup from hand to hand.

LV.
Pinocchio Finally Ceases To Be A Marionette And Becomes A Boy

I've watched a lot of movies, but I've never seen one being filmed. I don't know if this production was similar to *The Count of Monte Cristo*, or *The Shanghai Express*, but I sort of doubt it. Arlis and I stayed on the office steps and watched. We tried to be quiet but it didn't take long to realize the Hollywood we were watching was filmed on a slapstick backlot in 1932.

My brother Bruno is no director and I swear his knowledge of pictures goes no further than baseball cards, but he stood behind the girl with the camera telling her exactly how everything should look.

In front of them, Pinocchio waited, seated on the silvery grill of a car for sale. He looked like a toy on a shelf.

Tic Toc held a big white cue card with Pinocchio's lines. I'm sure Bruno had agonized over those words. I read them and rolled my eyes. *Hello. My name is Pinocchio. Remember me? I can never tell a lie. Geppetto Auto Repairs is the best.* I finished my coffee and grimaced.

"Okay!" Bruno called out. "Let's try it one more time. Toc, hold that sign up! You ready, Pinocchio?"

Pinocchio waved happily.

"You start filming now," Bruno told the girl with the camera and he yelled, "Action!"

Everyone stared at Pinocchio. He grinned and swung his feet.

"What are you doing?" Bruno screamed. "Read the lines!"

Tic Toc shook the big sign.

"Oh dear," Pinocchio said.

Bruno stomped his foot. "What? What's *oh dear* mean?"

The puppet mumbled, "I can't read."

"What?!"

"I never learned to read!" Pinocchio wailed. "In Italy, I only went to school a little bit." He held up his hand as if pinching salt.

Bruno swung a look at me, "You never told me he can't read!"

I shrugged.

Pinocchio cried, "I should have stayed in school!"

"Forget it!" Bruno roared. "We do it without the card." He approached poor Pinocchio. "Listen to me. You repeat what I tell you, okay?"

Pinocchio sniffled. "Okay…"

"I tell you what to say."

Pinocchio nodded.

Bruno read the cue card out loud and asked, "You got that?"

Pinocchio nodded.

"Okay. Angela let's try it again." He tapped her on the shoulder and she began to film. "Action!" he yelled.

"Hello," the puppet began. "I'm Pinocchio. Geppetto Auto Repair is the best."

"Cut!" Bruno stomped and bellowed, "What about the *I never tell a lie* part? You have to say that!"

Pinocchio threw his wooden hands over his mouth.

"Try it again!" Bruno ordered. "Action!"

We all watched Pinocchio as he spoke, "I'm Pinocchio. I try not to lie. Geppetto—"

"Cut! What do you mean you *try* not to lie?

Say, *I never tell a lie!*" Bruno pounded his fist into his other hand. "Angela, you tell him the line. Maybe he will listen to you." Bruno turned his back on Pinocchio and glared at the blue sky above.

I felt terrible for Pinocchio. I wanted to run down there and help, but being on the stairs gave me a safe distance from that calamity, like looking out a window at a sinking ship.

When they were done practicing, they tried again.

Bruno looked ready to throw a car if it didn't work. He took a deep breath and hollered, "Action!"

I clutched the railing and prayed for that poor little nervous puppet.

"Hello…My name is Pinocchio. Remember me?" he squeaked. I thought he couldn't go on, but he did. "I can never tell a lie." He gasped and covered his nose dramatically. "Geppetto Auto Repairs is the best." Then suddenly, right through his fingers, his nose grew. It was long as a yardstick.

"Cut!" Bruno shouted. "That's it! We're done!"

Pinocchio cried and kicked his feet and dented the clay chromed bumper.

As I hopped off the stairs I ran past the sound of Tic Toc tearing the cue card in half. I don't know who was more upset, between Pinocchio's sobbing and my brother's ranting.

Bruno wheeled me around with his strong hand. "I thought you said he couldn't lie!"

"That's what he told me." I shook myself free of him. "He's just a boy."

"He's a stupid puppet!" Bruno screamed.

While he wrestled the camera from Angela, I hurried to the car Pinocchio was slumped on, racked with tears. He was really worked up. With the bright spotlight still on him, he resembled his countryman, Pagliacci.

"Pinocchio," I said, "Pinocchio…" I touched his shoulder and he jumped.

"Oh!" he sobbed. "I don't like this job! I'd rather be a donkey again!" so sincere and heartfelt, his nose had grown back to its previous size. Then he gripped my arm tightly. "Take me back to the circus! Let's go now! We have to leave this place!"

I pictured us doing that. I saw us leaving the Auto Repair and the alley and this town, and driving fast as we could back to Louise.

I lifted him off the car and patted his little back.

I didn't know what we were going to do.

It was only morning, the day was still waiting. If I could say something to make him feel better, I would.

PINOCCHIO IN AMERICA
Written by Allen Frost
September 2015—May 2016

Books by Good Deed Rain

Saint Lemonade, Allen Frost, 2014. Two novels illustrated by the author in the manner of the old Big Little Books.

Playground, Allen Frost, 2014. Poems collected from seven years of chapbooks.

Roosevelt, Allen Frost, 2015. A Pacific Northwest novel set in July, 1942, when a boy and a girl search for a missing elephant. Illustrated throughout by Fred Sodt.

5 Novels, Allen Frost, 2015. Novels written over five years, featuring circus giants, clockwork animals, detectives and time travelers.

The Sylvan Moore Show, Allen Frost, 2015. A short story omnibus of 193 stories written over 30 years.

Town in a Cloud, Allen Frost, 2015. A 3 part book of poetry, written during the Bellingham rainy seasons of fall, winter, and spring.

A Flutter of Birds Passing Through Heaven: A Tribute to Robert Sund. 2016. Edited by Allen Frost and Paul Piper. The story of a legendary Ish River poet & artist.

At the Edge of America, Allen Frost, 2016. Two novels in one book blend time travel in a mythical poetic America.

Lake Erie Submarine, Allen Frost, 2016. A two week vacation in Ohio inspired these poems, illustrated by the author.

and Light, Paul Piper, 2016. Poetry written over three years. Illustrated with watercolors by Penny Piper.

The Book of Ticks, Allen Frost, 2017. A giant collection of 8 mysterious adventures featuring Phil Ticks. Illustrated throughout by Aaron Gunderson.

I Can Only Imagine, Allen Frost, 2017. Five adventures of love and heartbreak dreamed in an imaginary world. Cover & color illustrations by Annabelle Barrett.

The Orphanage of Abandoned Teenagers, Allen Frost, 2017. A fictional guide for teens and their parents. Illustrated by the author.

In the Valley of Mystic Light: An Oral History of the Skagit Valley Arts Scene, 2017. Edited by Claire Swedberg & Rita Hupy.

Different Planet, Allen Frost, 2017. Four science fiction adventures: reincarnation, robots, talking animals, outer space and clones. Cover & illustrations by Laura Vasyutynska.

Go with the Flow: A Tribute to Clyde Sanborn. 2018. Edited by Allen Frost. The life and art of a timeless river poet.

Homeless Sutra, Allen Frost, 2018. Four stories: Sylvan Moore, a flying monk, a water salesman, and a guardian rabbit.

The Lake Walker, Allen Frost 2018. A little novel set in black and white like one of those old European movies about death and life.

A Hundred Dreams Ago, Allen Frost, 2018. A winter book of poetry and prose. Illustrated by Aaron Gunderson.

Almost Animals, Allen Frost, 2018. A collection of linked stories, thinking about what makes us animals.

The Robotic Age, Allen Frost, 2018. A vaudeville magician and his faithful robot track down ghosts. Illustrated throughout by Aaron Gunderson.

Kennedy, Allen Frost, 2018. This sequel to Roosevelt is a coming-of-age fable set during two weeks in 1962 in a mythical Kennedy-land. Illustrated throughout by Fred Sodt.

Fable, Allen Frost, 2018. There's something going on in this country and I can best relate it in fable: the parable of the rabbits, a bedtime story, and the diary of our trip to Ohio.

Elbows & Knees: Essays & Plays, Allen Frost, 2018. A thrilling collection of writing about some of my favorite subjects, from B-movies to Brautigan.

The Last Paper Stars, Allen Frost 2019. A trip back in time to the 20 year old mind of Frankenstein, and two other worlds of the future.

Walt Amherst is Awake, Allen Frost, 2019. The dreamlife of an office worker. Illustrated throughout by Aaron Gunderson.

When You Smile You Let in Light, Allen Frost, 2019. An atomic love story written by a 23 year old.

Pinocchio in America, Allen Frost, 2019. After 82 years buried underground, Pinocchio returns to life behind a car repair shop in America.

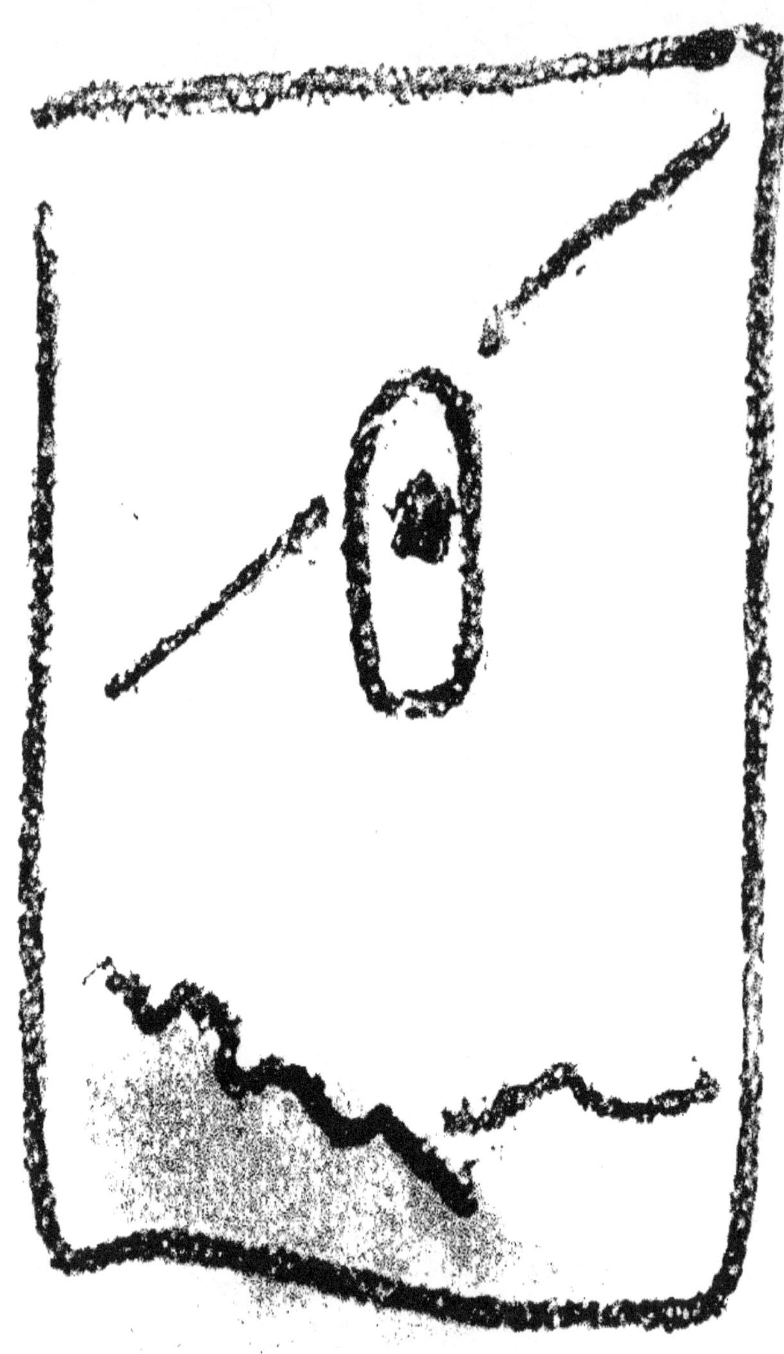

"I can take you there."